喚醒你的英文語感 ！

Get a Feel for English !

喚醒你的英文語感！

Get a Feel for English !

Overheard in a Taxi
雙語計程車
英文句典

附
**中英親聲
講解音檔**

編著 ◎ 劉怡均

⊕ 雙語溝通懶人包　　🚌 萬用情境聊天話題　　▣ Uber專區

Where can I take you? No problem! The journey will take about twenty minutes. Let me open the trunk. We're almost there. Here we are. Sorry, Taiwan dollars only. Have a nice day.

　　有搭過計程車的朋友們就知道，會發生在計程車上的對話，哪一句不是極為生活化的聊天用語呢？換句話說，這本書的出發點雖然是寫給計程車司機，幫助司機們與外國乘客溝通無礙的英文工具書，但只要是想要輕鬆學習英文的讀者，本書絕對會讓你感到親切又實用。

　　從事英文教學十多年，看著學生從不會到會，像在坐雲霄飛車——開車的是學生，坐車的是我！無論學生有什麼疑難雜症，風雨同舟，在不斷見招拆招的過程中，我們手拉著手一起收穫珍貴的成果，教學相長。但是，寫書就完全是另外一回事了。身為編著者，我看不見讀者，讀者在閱讀過程中產生的內心掙扎小劇場，我幫不上忙。因此，當初在規劃架構時，我就決定，一定要另外錄製中英雙語講解來幫助讀者更熟悉句型，而此設計也成為本書的特點之一。

　　對於平日工作繁忙的讀者，需要短時間內高效學習，推薦必先閱讀的章節是第一章「關於乘客的需求」，內容包含溝通目的地、客人趕時間、客人的搭乘要求、客人常說的話等主題，有助於預先掌握常見情形，立即運用在工作與生活中。有時間慢慢學習的時候，則可進一步探索第二章與第三章，內容包括從乘客攔車／叫車、上車（放行李）、目的地、行車路線、收費到下車等整個過程中所有必備語句，以及行車途中若需要輕鬆攀談的萬用小聊天範例（珍奶、故宮、夜市、名勝古蹟、球賽等），讀完必定能使英語聊天能力大為增長！此外，本書也收錄了 Uber

專區，以及路上可能發生的特殊情境（遇到警察臨檢、「馬路三寶」、車禍事故等），方便讀者依照實際需求學習所需語句。

最重要的是，本書特別規劃「火速救援篇」，除了作為暖身之外，主要的用意是提供讀者「現學現賣」的基礎短句，全都是從書中挑選出的精華中之精華，萬一才剛購買本書就馬上載到外國乘客，本篇內容必可協助解決燃眉之急！

只要有心學習，每天花一點零碎時間，放輕鬆跟著我的講解音檔練習，開口說英文真的比你想像中還要簡單許多喔！

Nana 劉怡均

★ Nana 老師的英語口說小教室 ★　　　　　　🎧 MP3 **BONUS**

在正式開始本書精采內容之前，編著者有話跟你說⋯⋯
滿滿學習好物，錯過可惜！
音軌主題：
_Bonus-1　提升口語能力的妙招── Shadowing「跟讀法」
_Bonus-2　Guabao is 刈包！台灣專有名詞直接唸中文就 OK
_Bonus-3　用英文打招呼──隨性 or 有禮的差別
_Bonus-4　Get 口語上的發音變化，英文聽力一起進步！

CONTENTS

Chapter 3

**萬用
聊天話題**

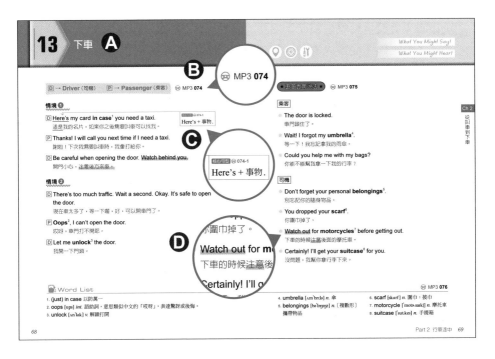

Ⓐ 主題：各單元皆以跨頁呈現，內容包含情境對話、實用說法和重點
字詞。

Ⓑ 音軌編號：以對話、例句或字彙區分為一軌，讀者可播放聆聽發音
並做跟讀練習。

Ⓒ 「核心句型」：編著者親聲錄製中英雙語講解，用聊天般的口吻深入
淺出，聽完就會。

Ⓓ 「實用短語」：中英雙語對照標記，不僅一目瞭然，更能加深印象。

MP3 **000**

還來不及將書裡的句子學到朗朗上口就載到外國客人？
別擔心！此暖身篇就是幫助司機朋友們秒解決問題的懶人包，
每天多看幾眼，從客人上車、簡短閒聊到收費送客一路暢通！

1. 問候

Hello. 哈囉！

Good morning. 早安！

How are you? 你好嗎？

2. 客人，你要去哪裡？

Yeah? 去哪？

Where to? 要去哪？

Where can I take you? 你要去哪裡？

3. 放行李

Let me open the trunk. 我開後車廂。

4. 確認目的地

National Taiwan University, right? 要去台大，對嗎？

5. 確認路線

Is Heping East Road okay? 走和平東路好嗎？

6. 詢問溫度

Is the temperature okay? 溫度還可以嗎？

7. 告知預估時間

It'll take about twenty minutes. 差不多要二十分鐘。

8. 靠近目的地

We're almost there. 我們快到了。

9. 抵達目的地

Is here okay? 這邊停車可以嗎？

Here we are. 我們到囉。

10. 車費

OK. Two hundred, please. 好。麻煩，兩百元。

Your change. 找錢給你。

11. 聽不懂時

Excuse me? 不好意思（你剛說什麼）？

What was that? 你剛剛說什麼？

Sorry, say that again? 抱歉，再說一次。

12. 肯定回答

Okay. 好的。

Got it. 了解。

No problem. 沒問題。

13. 否定回答

I'm sorry. 抱歉。

I don't know. 我不知道。

Sorry, cash only. 不好意思，只收現金。

Sorry, Taiwan dollars only. 不好意思，只收台幣。

14. 道歉

My bad. 都是我不好。

Sorry about that. 真是不好意思。

15. 道謝

Thanks. 謝囉。

Thanks a lot. 謝謝。

Thank you very much. 非常謝謝你。

16. 安撫乘客

Hold on. 別急。

Don't worry. 別擔心。

17. 提醒乘客

Be careful (opening the door). 開門小心。

Watch behind you. 注意後方來車。

Don't forget your umbrella/bag/phone. 別忘了你的雨傘／包包／手機。

19. 道別

Goodbye. 再見。

Take care. 保重。

20. 聊天

I recommend ... 我推薦……

It's very special. 很特別。

It's my favorite. 是我的最愛。

You will like it. 你會喜歡的。

Chapter 1

關於乘客的需求

如果句子不夠用，記得平時閱讀時，
可預先標出你認為可能會派上用場的句子，
這樣當遇到類似情境時一翻就到，迅速解決溝通問題！

D → **Driver**（司機）　　P → **Passenger**（乘客）　　☎ MP3 **001**

情境❶

D Good evening! Where are you going?

您好！您要去哪裡？

P I'd like to go to Lungshan **Temple**[1].

我要去龍山寺。

情境❷

D Hello! What's your **destination**[2]?

您好！今天要去哪裡？

P To Zhongxiao Fuxing MRT **Station**[3], please.

到忠孝復興捷運站，謝謝。

情境❸

D Hi there! Where can I take you?

嗨！要去哪兒？

P Can you take me to this **address**[4]?

可以載我到這個地址嗎？

🔋 Word List

1. temple [ˈtɛmpl] *n.* 廟
2. destination [ˌdɛstəˈneʃən] *n.* 目的地
3. station [ˈsteʃən] *n.* 車站
4. address [ˈædˌrɛs] *n.* 住址；地址

Ch 1

關於乘客的需求

★ 更多實用說法 ★　 MP3 **002**

司機

● Where are you **headed**[5]/going?

您要去哪裡？

● Where to?

要去哪兒？

乘客

● To Taipei 101, please.

到台北101，謝謝。

● Could you take me to Taipei Songshan **Airport**[6]?

你能載我到台北松山機場嗎？

● I need to go to Taipei Main Station, please.

我要去台北車站，謝謝。

● Could you drive me to the **intersection**[7] of Zhongxiao East **Road**[8] and Keelung Road?

你能載我到忠孝東路跟基隆路的那個路口嗎？

　MP3 **003**

5. head [hɛd] *v.* 朝某特定方向前往
6. airport [ˈɛr.port] *n.* 機場
7. intersection [ˌɪntəˈsɛkʃən] *n.* 十字路口
8. road [rod] *n.* 路

| D → **Driver**（司機） | P → **Passenger**（乘客） | 🎧 MP3 **004** |

情境 1

D Where can I take you?

今天想去哪裡呢？

P Where can I get the best night view in Taipei?

台北哪裡看夜景最棒呢？

D I **recommend**[1] the Taipei 101 **Observatory**[2].

我推薦去台北 101 觀景台。

> 核心句型 🎧 004-1
> I recommend +
> 地點.

情境 2

D Where would you like to go?

您想去哪裡？

P Can you take me to a night market where I can walk around?

帶我去一個可以四處走走的夜市。

D Sure, for a casual walk, you can go to Shilin Night Market.

沒問題，如果是要散散步，可以去士林夜市。

> 核心句型 🎧 004-2
> You can go to + 地點.

 Word List

1. recommend [ˌrɛkəˈmɛnd] *v.* 推薦
2. observatory [əbˈzɝvəˌtorɪ] *n.* 觀景台；天文台

★更多實用說法★ 🎧 MP3 **005**

乘客

- I'd like to go shopping.
  我想去逛街。

- I want to go clubbing tonight.
  今晚我想去夜店。

- I need to buy some **souvenirs**[3] before heading to the airport.
  在去機場之前，我需要買一些紀念品。

- I want to go to the nearest beach to enjoy the sunset.
  我想去最近的海灘欣賞夕陽。

- Please take me to a local restaurant to try **authentic**[4] Taiwanese food.
  請帶我去一家在地的餐廳，品嚐正宗的台灣美食。

司機

- Sure, no problem.
  好的，沒問題。

- I'll take you to Heping Island.
  我載你到和平島。

🎧 MP3 **006**

---

3. souvenir [ˋsuvəˌnɪr] *n.* 紀念品
4. authentic [ɔˋθɛntɪk] *adj.* 正宗的；真正的；可靠的；可信的

D → **Driver**（司機）　　P → **Passenger**（乘客）　⚙ MP3 **007**

情境 ❶

P Hi, can you take me to the night market **nearby**[1]?

嗨，你能載我到附近的夜市嗎？

D Sure! Just tell me where to go.

好！告訴我怎麼走。

P Go **straight**[2] for a while, and then at the next intersection, make a right turn.

先直走一下下，然後下一個十字路口右轉。

情境 ❷

P I think we need to turn **left**[3] at some point.

等一下應該是要左轉。

D No problem. Just tell me where to turn.

沒問題，要左轉的時候跟我說。

P Keep going straight and turn left at the next traffic light.

先繼續直行，然後下一個紅綠燈左轉。

 Word List

1. **nearby** [ˈnɪrˌbaɪ] *adj./adv.* 附近的；在附近
2. **straight** [stret] *adj./adv.* 筆直的；一直
3. **left** [lɛft] *adv./adj./n.* 向左；左方的；左邊

★ 更多實用說法 ★ 🔊 MP3 **008**

司機

● We're **almost**[4] there.
我們差不多快要到了。

● Where would you like me to drop you off?
你想要在哪個地方下車？

乘客

● Keep going straight for a while.
先繼續直行。

● It's on the left/**right**[5].
是在左邊／右邊。

● **Turn**[6] around, and then go all the way to the end.
迴轉，然後直走到底。

● Please drop me off at the traffic light.
請讓我在紅綠燈那邊下車。

● Take the first right after the hospital.
醫院之後第一個路口右轉。

🔊 MP3 **009**

---

4. **almost** [ˈɔlˌmost] *adv.* 幾乎；差一點；將近
5. **right** [raɪt] *adv./adj./n.* 向右；右方的；右邊

6. **turn** [tɜn] *n./v.* 轉彎

04 客人趕時間

D → **Driver**（司機）   P → **Passenger**（乘客）   ⊙ MP3 **010**

情境 ❶

P I'm running late for a meeting. Downtown, please!

我開會要遲到了。麻煩到市中心！

口語也可唸作 ASAP

D No worries, we'll get you there as soon as possible.

沒問題，我會盡快載你到目的地。

情境 ❷

P Hey, I'm in a rush. I need to get to the airport. I think I might **miss**[1] my **flight**[2].

嗨，我趕時間，要馬上到機場。我很可能會錯過我的班機。

D No problem! Which **terminal**[3] are you heading to?

沒問題！哪一個航廈？

P Terminal 1. My flight leaves in less than an hour.

第一航廈。我的班機再不到一個小時就要起飛了。

D I'll take the quickest **route**[4]. We'll get you there in no time.

我會走最快的路線，會很快送你到機場。

 Word List

1. miss [mɪs] v. 未趕上；錯過
2. flight [flaɪt] n. 班機；飛機班次
3. terminal [ˈtɝmən]] n. 航廈；總站
4. route [rut] n. 路線

★ 更多實用說法 ★　 MP3 **011**

乘客

- I have to be there in 15 minutes.
  我必須在十五分鐘內抵達目的地。

- The **train**[5] leaves at 10 o'clock.
  火車十點開。

- I'm in a hurry.
  我趕時間。

- Could you drive faster, please?
  能麻煩你開快一點嗎？

- Do you know any **shortcuts**[6]?
  你知不知道有什麼比較近的路線？

司機

- It's always like this at this hour.
  這個時段車況都是這樣的。

- Of course, I'll get you there as fast as I can.
  沒問題，我盡快。

- Don't worry, I'll do my best.
  別擔心，我盡力。

 MP3 **012**

---

5. train [tren] *n.* 火車
6. shortcut [ˋʃɔrtˌkʌt] *n.* 捷徑；近路

D → **Driver**（司機）　P → **Passenger**（乘客）　🎧 MP3 **013**

情境 ❶

P Excuse me, I'm not feeling well. Could you pull over?

不好意思，我不舒服，能請你靠邊停車嗎？

D I'll find a safe **spot**[1] to stop. Just give me a second.

我找地方靠邊停，稍等一下。

情境 ❷

P Excuse me, shouldn't you have turned left?

不好意思，你剛剛是不是應該要左轉？

D Sorry, no left turn here.

抱歉，這裡禁止左轉。

P It seems like you're going the wrong way.

你好像開錯路了。

D Don't worry. I'll find a **suitable**[2] place to make a U-turn.

別擔心。我等一下會找地方迴轉。

 Word List

1. **spot** [spɑt] *n./v.* 場所；地點；看見　　2. **suitable** [ˋsutəbl] *adj.* 合適的

★更多實用說法★ 🔊 MP3 **014**

乘客

◦ Are we on the right track?

我們有走對路嗎？

◦ Just want to make sure.

只是想要確認一下。

◦ I'm **carsick**[3].

我有點暈車。

司機

◦ Don't worry. I know where I'm going.

別擔心，我知道怎麼走。

◦ Sorry about that! I must have missed that turn.

抱歉！我剛剛一定是錯過了。

◦ Sorry, there's a speed camera.

不好意思，那邊有測速照相機。

核心句型 🔊 014-1

There is/are + 事物.

◦ That was a one-way **street**[4].

這是單行道。

◦ I took a wrong turn. My bad!

我剛剛轉錯彎了，對不起！

🔊 MP3 **015**

3. carsick [`kar͵sɪk] *adj.* 暈車的

4. street [strit] *n.* 街

21

D → Driver（司機）　　P → Passenger（乘客）　　🎧 MP3 **016**

情境 ❶

P Can you turn up the A/C? It's a bit hot.

能麻煩你把空調開大一點嗎？車裡有點熱。

D Sure, no problem! Is this **temperature**[1] better for you now?

當然沒問題！現在溫度有好一點嗎？

P Much better, thank you!

好多了，謝謝！

情境 ❷

P Can you open the **window**[2]?

能麻煩你把窗戶打開嗎？

D **Certainly**[3]! Is that okay?

當然，這樣可以嗎？

P Yes, that's perfect. Thanks.

好，這樣很好。謝謝。

D You're welcome!

不客氣！

📇 Word List

1. temperature [ˈtɛmprətʃə] *n.* 溫度；氣溫
2. window [ˈwɪndo] *n.* 窗戶
3. certainly [ˈsɝtənlɪ] *adv.* 沒問題；肯定地

★ 更多實用說法 ★　🎧 MP3 **017**

乘客

● Could you **open**[4]/**close**[5] the window?
可以請你打開／關上窗戶嗎？

核心句型 🎧 017-1
Could you 禮貌地請求

● Could you turn up/down the air conditioning?
可以請你把空調開強／弱一點嗎？

● Could you turn the music down a bit?
可以請你把音樂關小聲點嗎？

司機

● Certainly! No problem!
當然！沒問題！

● Of course! I'll turn down the **volume**[6].
當然可以，我來調小聲一點。

● Is that better?
這樣有比較好嗎？

● Is it okay?
這樣可以嗎？

🎧 MP3 **018**

4. open [ˋopən] *v.* 打開
5. close [klos] *v.* 關上
6. volume [ˋvaljəm] *n.* 音量

⭐ 基本應對用語

☐ Can you take me to + 地點？
可以載我去……嗎？

☐ I want to go to + 地點.
我想要去……。

☐ I need to get to + 地點.
我要去……。

☐ Grand Hyatt Taipei, please.
到台北君悅酒店，謝謝。

> 核心句型 🎧 019-1
> 地點, please.

☐ I'm in a hurry/rush.
我趕時間。

☐ Are we almost there?
請問快到了嗎？

☐ Please turn around.
麻煩你掉頭。

> 核心句型 🎧 019-2
> Would you mind doing + 某事？

☐ Would you mind turning the music volume down?
你介意把音樂音量轉小聲一點嗎？

☐ Can you let me off here?
可以讓我在這裡下車嗎？

☐ This is me/it.
這邊停就可以。

☐ Thank you.
謝謝你。

司機　　🎧 MP3 **020**

☐ Where to ?
要去哪裡？

核心句型 🎧 020-1

_____ is a good choice.

☐ If you have time, Taipei 101 is a good choice.
如果你有時間，去台北 101 看看是個不錯的選擇。

☐ It will take about 20 minutes.
車程大概需要二十分鐘。

核心句型 🎧 020-2

It will take about ＋ 時間 .

☐ Is the temperature okay for you?
請問溫度這樣可以嗎？

☐ If you need anything, just tell me.
如果你有什麼需要，請隨時告訴我。

☐ Feel free to let me know.
有什麼需求，都可以隨時讓我知道。

☐ Sorry, I didn't get that.
不好意思，我剛剛沒聽懂你的意思。

☐ Could you say that again?
能麻煩你再說一遍嗎？

☐ Sure, no problem.
當然，沒有問題。

☐ Of course.
當然（沒有問題）。

☐ Thank you very much.
非常感謝你。

Notes

Chapter 2

從叫車到下車

Part 1

乘客叫車

01 路邊攔車

⊙ MP3 **021**

D → **Driver**（司機）　　P → **Passenger**（乘客）

情境 ❶

D Good morning! Where to?
早安，去哪裡呢？

P To Taipei City Hall.
到台北市政府。

D No problem.
沒問題。

情境 ❷

D Hello! Where can I take you today?
你好！今天要去哪裡呢？

P I need to get to the Sheraton **Hotel**[1], please.
請送我到喜來登大飯店。

D Sure! Just hop in.
沒問題！請上車。

 Word List

1. hotel [ho`tɛl] *n.* 旅館；飯店

★更多實用說法★ 🎧 MP3 **022**

司機

● Hi, your destination, please.
嗨，請告訴我你的目的地。

● Where do you need to go?
您要去哪裡？

● Good evening! Where can I take you?
晚安，您要去哪裡呢？

乘客

● Taoyuan International Airport.
到桃園國際機場。

● Go that way.
走那條路。（*用手指示方向*）

● I'm going to the Nanjing Fuxing intersection.
我要去南京復興路口。

● Could you take me to Nangang **Exhibition**[2] Center?
你能載我到南港展覽館嗎？

> 核心句型 🎧 022-1
> Could you take me to + 地點？

🎧 MP3 **023**

2. exhibition [ˌɛksəˈbɪʃən] *n.* 展覽（會）

Part 1 乘客叫車　　*31*

02 電話叫車

D → **Driver**（司機）　　P → **Passenger**（乘客）　　☺ MP3 **024**

情境 ❶

P Hello, I need a **cab**[1], please. I'm at the Taipei World Trade Center.

嗨，我要叫車，我人現在在台北世貿中心。

D Sure, I'll be there in five **minutes**[2].

沒問題，我五分鐘內能到。

> 核心句型 ☺ 024-1
> I'll be there in + 時間.

情境 ❷

P Hi, may I book a **taxi**[3] at 10:00?

From Taipei Main Station to Taipei Songshan Airport.

嗨，我十點鐘可以訂一輛計程車嗎？

從台北車站到松山機場。

D OK, no problem! The car number is 865.

OK，車號是 865。

 Word List

1. cab [kæb] *n.* 計程車
2. minute [ˋmɪnɪt] *n.* 分鐘
3. taxi [ˋtæksɪ] *n.* 計程車

★ 更多實用說法 ★　　🔊 MP3 **025**

乘客

● I need a cab to The Grand Hotel.
我要叫車到圓山大飯店。

● I need a taxi at No. 3, Section 4, Zhongshan North Road.
我人在中山北路四段三號，我要叫車。

● Could you **send**[4] a taxi to + 地點 / 地址？
可以麻煩派一輛計程車到【地點 / 地址】嗎？

司機

● Your **location**[5], please?
您現在位置在哪裡呢？

● Your destination, please?
您的目的地是哪裡呢？

● I'll be there in about fifteen minutes.
我大概十五分鐘之內會到。

● I'll pick you up **shortly**[6].
我馬上過去接您。

🔊 MP3 **026**

4. send [sɛnd] *v.* 派遣
5. location [loˋkeʃən] *n.* 地點；位置
6. shortly [ˋʃɔrtlɪ] *adv.* 很快

D → **Driver**（司機）　　P → **Passenger**（乘客）　　☏ MP3 **027**

情境 ❶

P Could you open the **trunk**[1]? I need to put my **luggage**[2] in.
　麻煩打開後車廂好嗎？我要放行李。

D Sure! Let me open the trunk.
　沒問題！我來開後車廂。

> 核心句型 ☏ 027-1
> Let me + 做某事.

情境 ❷

P Will this fit in the trunk?
　這個放得進後車廂嗎？

D I'm sorry. There's no **room**[3] in the trunk.
　不好意思，後車廂沒有空間了。

Word List

1. trunk [trʌŋk] *n.* 後車廂
2. luggage [ˈlʌgɪdʒ] *n.* 行李
3. room [rum] *n.* 房間；空間

 MP3 **028**

司機

● Should I put your **bags**[4] in the trunk?
要幫你把行李放到後車廂嗎？

● Let me help you with that.
我幫你放那件行李。

乘客

● Can I put this in the front seat?
我可以把這個放在前座嗎？

● Please be careful. It's very **heavy**[5].
請小心，這個很重。

● It's okay. I'll take this **inside**[6] the car with me.
沒關係，我把行李帶上車。、

● Please keep this side up.
請保持這一面向上。

 MP3 **029**

4. bag [bæg] *n.* 袋子
5. heavy [ˈhɛvɪ] *adj.* 重的
6. inside [ˈɪnˈsaɪd] *adv./n.* 往裡面；內部

D → **Driver**（司機）　　P → **Passenger**（乘客）　　☎ MP3 **030**

情境 ❶

P To the **Museum**[1] of Contemporary Art, please.
麻煩到當代藝術館。

> 核心句型 ☎ 030-1
> Do you know +
> 事物？

D I'm sorry. I don't know where that is. <u>Do you know</u> the address?
不好意思，我不知道那個地方是哪裡。<u>你知道</u>地址嗎？

P Here, this is the address.
地址在這邊。

D Okay, just a second. Let me check the GPS.
好的，稍等，我看一下導航路線。

情境 ❷

P I need to go to Taipei Main Station.
我要到台北車站。

D No problem. Are you taking the High Speed Rail (THSR)?
沒問題，你要去搭高鐵嗎？

P Yeah!
對啊！

D Then I'll drop you off at East **Gate**[2] 3.
那我等一下讓你在東三門下車。

Word List

1. museum [mju`zɪəm] *n.* 博物館　　2. gate [get] *n.* 大門

★ 更多實用說法 ★　🎧 MP3 **031**

乘客

● I'm **meeting**³ a friend at the West **Entrance**⁴.
　我要在西側入口和朋友會面。

● Can you drop me off there?
　你可以在那裡讓我下車嗎？

司機

● Which entrance do you want?
　你要去哪個入口呢？

● Of course! The main gate?
　當然可以！大門口（正門口）嗎？

● OK. Here's the intersection. Which way from here?
　好，這邊就是十字路口了，再來往哪邊走呢？

● Is that on Huaxi Street?
　那是在華西街嗎？

🎧 MP3 **032**

3. **meet** [mit] *v.* 遇見；和……會面　　4. **entrance** [ˈɛntrəns] *n.* 入口

D → **Driver**（司機）　　P → **Passenger**（乘客）　　😊 MP3 **033**

情境 ①

P To Chiang Kai-shek **Memorial**[1] Hall.

到中正紀念堂。

D Sure! How would you like to go?

好的！想怎麼走？

P Oh, I have no idea. Just the **quickest**[2] route.

噢，我不知道路，最快的路線就好。

D Okay.

好的。

情境 ②

D Do you want me to take the **elevated**[3] road or **surface**[4] streets?

你要我走高架道路還是平面道路呢？

P Take the elevated road, please.

走高架，麻煩了。

Word List

1. memorial [mə`morɪəl] *adj.* 紀念的　　3. elevated [`ɛləˌvetɪd] *adj.* 高層的

2. quickest [`kwɪkəst] *adj.* 最快的　　4. surface [`sɝfɪs] *adj.* 地面上的

★ 更多實用說法 ★ 🎧 MP3 **034**

司機

● How would you like to go?
您想要怎麼走？

● Is Xinyi Road okay?
走信義路可以嗎？

● Do you have a **preferred**[5] route?
你有偏好的路線嗎？

乘客

● I'll leave it up to you.
交給你決定就好。

● I don't mind.
我無所謂。

● I think Zhongshan North Road is **faster**[6].
我覺得中山北路比較快。

🎧 MP3 **035**

5. preferred [prɪˋfɜd] *adj.* 偏好的；更合意的
6. faster [ˋfæstə] *adj.* 比較快的

基本應對用語

☐ Good morning. Where can I take you?
　早安，你要去哪裡？

☐ Good afternoon. Where are you going?
　午安，你要去哪裡？

☐ Good evening. Where are you headed?
　晚安，你要去哪裡？

☐ Hi there, your destination?
　嗨，你要去哪裡？

☐ Sure thing. ╱ Sure, no problem!
　當然。╱ 當然，沒問題！

☐ Let me help you with your bags.
　我來幫你放你的行李。

☐ Please fasten your seatbelt.
　請繫好安全帶。

☐ Do you know the address?
　你知道地址嗎？

☐ How would you like to go?
　你想怎麼走？

☐ I'm sorry to have kept you waiting.
　不好意思讓你等了一會兒。

乘客　　 MP3 **037**

☐ I need to go to the Taipei Arena.
我要去台北小巨蛋。

☐ Taipei Dome, please.
請載我到台北大巨蛋。

☐ Take me here.
載我到這裡。（把地址遞給司機）

☐ Take me to the nearest MRT station, please.
請載我到最近的捷運車站，謝謝。

☐ I'm going to this place.
我要去這個地方。

☐ I'm heading to Daan Park.
我要去大安森林公園。

☐ Please go to Huashan Creative Park first and I will tell you how to go from there.
請先到華山那邊，我會再告訴你接著怎麼走。

☐ Hello, I need a cab to Taipei Garden Hotel.
哈囉！我要叫一輛車到台北花園大酒店。

☐ Could you help me with my luggage?
你可以幫我放一下行李嗎？

☐ I'm not in a hurry. Take your time.
我不趕時間，你慢慢開沒關係。

Notes

Part 2

行車途中

☎ MP3 **038**

turn left
左轉

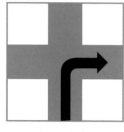

turn right
右轉

go straight
直走

go straight to the end
直走到底

cross[1] the bridge
穿過橋

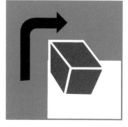

go around the corner
繞過轉角

Ch 2

從叫車到下車

乘客

- Stay in the left lane. 保持在左側車道。
- Get in the right lane. 開到右側車道。
- Turn right at the next intersection, please.
  下個路口請右轉。
- Go straight for two **blocks**².
  往前開兩個路口。
- Go straight to the end of this road, and then turn left.
  繼續開這條路到底，然後左轉。
- Please go straight until you **reach**³ the **roundabout**⁴.
  請直直開到圓環路口。
- Keep going until you see the post office.
  一直開，直到你看到郵局。
- Just go around the **corner**⁵, and you'll find the entrance to the
  building⁶.
  拐一個彎，就可以看到大樓入口。

Word List　MP3 **040**

1. **cross** [krɔs] *v.* 穿過；橫跨
2. **block** [blɑk] *n.* 街口
3. **reach** [ritʃ] *v.* 抵達
4. **roundabout** [ˈraʊndəˌbaʊt] *n.* 圓環
5. **corner** [ˈkɔrnɚ] *n.* 轉角
6. **building** [ˈbɪldɪŋ] *n.* 建築物

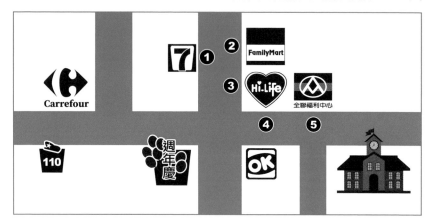

🔊 MP3 **041**　　　　更多地點／設施的英文說法見第 174 頁

❶ 7-ELEVEN is on the left.

7-ELEVEN 便利商店在左手邊。

❷ FamilyMart is on the right.

全家便利商店在右手邊。

❸ Hi-Life convenience store is at/on the corner.

萊爾富便利商店就在轉角。

❹ Hi-Life is **across**[1] from OKmart.

萊爾富就在 OK 便利商店對面。

❺ PX Mart is two blocks away from Carrefour.

全聯距離家樂福兩個街口。

 Word List

1. across [əˋkrɔs] *prep.* 在……的對面

★ 更多實用說法 ★　🎧 MP3 **042**

乘客

● You can't miss it.
你一定看得到。

● You'll see the shopping mall <u>on the left/right</u>.
購物中心就<u>在左邊 / 右邊</u>。

● Go straight until you see 7-ELEVEN <u>on the left-hand side</u>.
直走，直到你看到 7-ELEVEN，目的地<u>在左手邊</u>。

● It's right at the corner of the street.
就在這條街的轉角。

● It's **behind**[2] the police station.
就在警察局後面。

● To get to the City Hall, you'll need to go two blocks **beyond**[3] the school.
要到市政府，過了學校還要兩個街口。

🎧 MP3 **043**

2. behind [bɪ`haɪnd] *prep.* 在⋯⋯的後面
3. beyond [bɪ`jɑnd] *prep.* 超過；更遠於

MP3 **044**

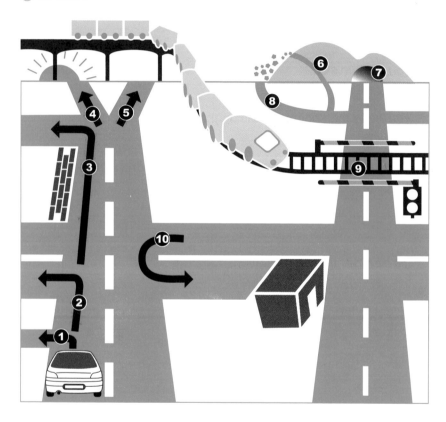

- ❶ 1st left 第一個路口左轉
- ❷ 2nd left 第二個路口左轉
- ❸ 3rd left 第三個路口左轉
- ❹ go left 走左邊
- ❺ go right 走右邊
- ❻ go up the hill 開上山
- ❼ tunnel 隧道
- ❽ curve 彎道
- ❾ railroad crossing 鐵路平交道
- ❿ U-turn 迴轉

★ 更多實用說法 ★　🎧 MP3 **045**

乘客

● Turn left at the traffic lights.
　紅綠燈左轉。

● **Pass**[1] through the **tunnel**[2], and you'll see the **park**[3] on your left.
　穿過隧道，公園在你的左手邊。

● Stay toward the right at the **fork**[4].
　繼續往雙叉路右邊開。

● At the fork, take the right lane.
　在雙叉口處，請走右邊的車道。

● Take the second right after the gas station.
　看到加油站之後的第二個路口右轉。

● Please go left at the next **junction**[5].
　請在下一個路口左轉。

● At the intersection, make a right turn.
　在十字路口右轉。

 Word List　🎧 MP3 **046**

1. **pass** [pæs] *v.* 經過；路過
2. **tunnel** [ˈtʌnl] *n.* 隧道
3. **park** [pɑrk] *n.* 公園
4. **fork** [fɔrk] *n.* 雙叉口
5. **junction** [ˈdʒʌŋkʃən] *n.* 交叉路口
　（美式常用 intersection）

04 確認駕駛路線 A

情境 ❶

Ｐ Turn left here.

這邊左轉。

Ｄ I can't turn left here. I have to come from the other **direction**[1].

這邊禁止左轉。我要從另外一邊繞回來。

情境 ❷

Ｐ Pass the gas station and then make a U-turn.

經過加油站之後迴轉。

Ｄ There's a no U-turn **sign**[2]. I'll have to go around.

這邊禁止迴轉，我要繞一下。

Ｐ Okay.

好。

 Word List

1. direction [dəˋrɛkʃən] *n.* 方向
2. sign [saɪn] *n.* 標誌；告示牌

★ 更多實用說法 ★　　🎧 MP3 **048**

司機

- Left turns are only allowed after 8 o'clock.
  這裡八點以後才可以左轉。

- Let me go up a little further.
  我再往前開一點。

- I can make a **U-turn**[3] at the next intersection.
  下一個十字路口我可以迴轉。

- I can take the expressway if you're in a rush.
  如果你趕時間的話，我可以走快速道路。

乘客

- Not this one. The next one.
  不是這個（路口）。下一個。

- Turn into the **alley**[4] and go all the way to the end.
  轉進巷子裡然後直走到底。

- Can you turn around and go back?
  你可以掉頭回去嗎？

🎧 MP3 **049**

3. U-turn [ˈjutɜn] *n.* 迴轉
4. alley [ˈælɪ] *n.* 巷子

D → **Driver** (司機)　　P → **Passenger** (乘客)　　☺ MP3 **050**

情境 ❶

D The road is **blocked**[1]. I have to turn around.
這條路封了，我要掉頭。

P How long will it take?
要多久時間啊？

D I'm not sure, but I think it won't take more than ten minutes.
我不確定，但是我想應該不會超過十分鐘。

P That's fine.
好吧。

情境 ❷

D There's a **parade**[2], and the roads are closed. I'll need to take a different route.
前面有遊行，路都封了，我要繞路。

P How much longer will it take?
還會花多長時間呢？

D Hard to say, but I'll do my best.
很難講，但我盡力而為。

🔖 Word List

1. blocked [blakt] *adj.* 受阻的；被堵塞的
2. parade [pə`red] *n.* 遊行

52

★更多實用說法★ 🎧 MP3 **051**

司機

- Sorry, we're **stuck**[3] in traffic.
  不好意思，現在塞車。

- We've got a parade coming up, and the roads are closed.
  有遊行，這邊的路都被封鎖了。

- Sorry for the **inconvenience**[4].
  造成不便很抱歉。

乘客

- I understand.
  我理解。

- It's okay. I'm not in a hurry.
  沒關係，我沒有在趕時間。

- You can drop me off at the nearest subway station.
  你可以讓我在最近的捷運站下車就好。

🎧 MP3 **052**

3. stuck [stʌk] *adj.* 卡住的；困住的
4. inconvenience [ˌɪnkənˈvinjəns] *n.* 不便；麻煩

D → **Driver**（司機）　　P → **Passenger**（乘客）　　😊 MP3 **053**

情境 ❶

P The place is just next to the MRT **exit**[1].

那個地方就在捷運出口旁邊。

> 核心句型 😊 053-1
> next to ＋ 地點

D Okay.

好的。

P Pull over here, please.

麻煩這裡靠邊停。

情境 ❷

P Can you **pull up**[2] a bit further?

可不可以停前面一點？

D No problem.

沒問題。

P Here's fine, thanks.

這邊就可以了，謝謝。

Word List

1. exit [ˈɛksɪt] *n.* 出口　　　　　2. pull up 停車

★ 更多實用說法 ★　🔊 MP3 **054**

司機

● We're almost there.
　差不多快要到了。

● The MRT station is coming up.
　捷運站快到了。

● Is here okay?
　這邊停可以嗎？

● It's just up ahead.
　就在前面。

乘客

● **Go through**[3] the intersection and then pull over.
　過十字路口停車。

● This is okay.
　這邊停就可以。

● Please let me off here.
　請讓我在這裡下車。

🔊 MP3 **055**

---

3. go through 穿越；經過

D → **Driver**（司機）　P → **Passenger**（乘客）　🎧 MP3 **056**

情境 ❶

D Okay. Here's the Zhongxiao Fuxing intersection.

好的，忠孝復興路口到了。

P On the right will be good. Thank you.

靠右邊停就好，謝謝。

情境 ❷

P Go around the corner, please.

可以轉過路口再停車嗎？麻煩你。

D It looks like there's an **accident**[1]. I'm not sure if I can drop you off there.

前面好像有交通事故，我不確定我可不可以讓你在那邊下車。

P Umm, it's okay. Just get as close as you can.

嗯，沒關係，盡量開近一點就好。

 Word List

1. accident [ˋæksədənt] *n.* 事故；意外事件

★ 更多實用說法 ★　🎧 MP3 **057**

司機

● Where do you want me to drop you off?
你要我讓你在哪裡下車？

● Do you want me to drop you off at a **specific**[2] location?
你要我把你送到某個特定的地點嗎？

乘客

● At the post office is fine.
郵局那裡就可以。

● Just past the intersection.
過十字路口就好。

● In **front**[3] of the department store.
百貨公司門口前。

● This is good. Stop the car here.
這邊就可以，這裡停車。

🎧 MP3 **058**

2. specific [spɪˈsɪfɪk] *adj.* 特定的

3. front [frʌnt] *n.* 前面；正面

D → **Driver**（司機）　P → **Passenger**（乘客）　🎧 MP3 **059**

情境 ❶

D Do you want **arrivals**¹ or **departures**²?

請問一下，你要到入境區還是出境區？

P Departures, please.

出境區，謝謝。

情境 ❷

D Which **airline**³ is it?

是哪一家航空公司呢？

P China Airlines.

華航。

D Have a **safe**⁴ and **pleasant**⁵ journey.

旅途平安愉快。

P **I appreciate**⁶ it! Will do, thanks!

好的。感謝你！謝謝！

 Word List　　🎧 MP3 **061**

1. arrival [əˈraɪvl] *n.* 抵達
2. departure [dɪˈpartʃə] *n.* 出發
3. airline [ˈɛrˌlaɪn] *n.* 航空公司
4. safe [sef] *adj.* 安全的
5. pleasant [ˈplɛzənt] *adj.* 令人愉快的
6. appreciate [əˈpriʃɪet] *v.* 感謝；欣賞

★更多實用說法★ 🎧 MP3 **060**

司機

● Is this the right terminal for your flight?

你的班機是這個航廈嗎？

● Is there anything else you need?

還有其他需要幫忙的地方嗎？

乘客

● Yeah, this is the right one. Thanks!

是的，是這裡沒錯。謝謝！

● Nah, I'm good. Thanks for asking though.

不用了，我這樣可以。還是謝謝你問我。

● EVA / United / Cathay Pacific.

長榮航空 / 聯合航空 / 國泰航空。

D → **Driver**（司機）　P → **Passenger**（乘客）　🎧 MP3 **062**

情境 ①

D **Here we are.** Tonghua (Linjiang) Street Night Market!
通化／臨江街夜市到囉！

P Sorry, can we **wait**[1] here? I need to pick up a friend.
不好意思，我們可以在這裡等一下嗎？我要接一個朋友。

D Sure, but I will leave the **meter**[2] running.
當然，但是我會繼續跳錶喔。

P That's fine. 沒關係。

情境 ②

P Can you pull over in front of the **bank**[3]? I need to pick up a friend.
你能不能在銀行前面靠邊停，我要接一個朋友上車。

D Sure!
好！

P Oh! My friend is there. He's the one in the blue **jacket**[4].
噢！我朋友在那邊，他穿藍色夾克。

D Okay, I see him.
好的，我看到他了。

🔋 Word List

1. wait [wet] *v.* 等待
2. meter [ˈmitə] *n.* 儀錶
3. bank [bæŋk] *n.* 銀行
4. jacket [ˈdʒækɪt] *n.* 夾克；外套

★ 更多實用說法 ★　🎧 MP3 **063**

司機

● Here we are.
我們到囉！

● We've **arrived**⁵ at your destination.
我們已經抵達你的目的地。

● Thank you for choosing our **service**⁶.
感謝搭乘。

乘客

● Perfect, thank you!
太棒了，謝謝！

● Thanks for getting me here.
謝謝你載我到這裡。

● It was nice talking to you.
跟你聊天很愉快。

🎧 MP3 **064**

5. arrive [əˋraɪv] *v.* 抵達
6. service [ˋsɝvɪs] *n.* 服務

10 抵達目的地 B

 → **Driver**（司機）　　 P → **Passenger**（乘客）　　 🛞 MP3 **065**

情境 ❶

P Oh no, I can't get my seatbelt off. It's stuck.
　天吶，我解不開安全帶，卡住了。

D Don't worry, let me help you with that.
　別擔心，我來幫你。

情境 ❷

D We've arrived at your destination. Would you like a **receipt**¹?
　我們已經抵達你的目的地了，你要收據嗎？

P Sure, a receipt would be great. Thanks for the **ride**².
　好啊，謝謝你。

D You're welcome. Need a hand with your luggage?
　不客氣。需要幫忙你搬行李嗎？

P No, I've got it. Thanks for asking.
　不用，我自己可以，謝謝你問我。

🔋 Word List

---

1. receipt [rɪˋsit] *n.* 收據　　　　　　2. ride [raɪd] *n.* 車程

★更多實用說法★　　🎧 MP3 **066**

司機

● Did you **enjoy**[3] your ride?
車程一路還愉快嗎？

● Need a hand with your bags?
需要我幫忙搬行李嗎？

乘客

● Sure, I'll take a receipt. Thanks.
當然，我要一張收據，謝謝。

● Yes, it was a pleasant ride.
是的，這趟車程很愉快。

● Sure, that would be great. Thank you!
當然，那就太好了，謝謝你！

● I think I'm good. Thanks.
我應該沒有其他需要。謝謝。

🎧 MP3 **067**

3. enjoy [ɪnˋdʒɔɪ] *v.* 欣賞；享受……的樂趣

11 車資收費 A

D → **Driver**（司機）　　**P** → **Passenger**（乘客）　😊 MP3 **068**

情境 ①

P I only have three hundred dollars (NT$300). Is that **enough**[1] to get to Hsinchu **Railway**[2] Station?

我身上只有三百元，到新竹火車站夠錢嗎？

D I'm not sure. Maybe about three hundred fifty (NT$350).

我不是很確定，可能差不多要三百五十元。

情境 ②

P Excuse me. Do you take US dollars?

不好意思，你有收美金嗎？

D No, sorry. Taiwan Dollars only.

沒有收美金，抱歉。只收台幣。

 Word List

1. **enough** [əˋnʌf] *adj.* 足夠的
2. railway [ˋrelˏwe] *n.* 鐵道

★ 更多實用說法 ★　🎧 MP3 **069**

乘客

- How much will it **cost**[3] to go to Taipei City Hall?
  到台北市政府要多少錢？

- Here's five hundred dollars (NT$500), keep the **change**[4].
  這裡是五百元，零錢不用找了。

- May I have a receipt, please?
  我可以要收據嗎？

司機

- It will cost about two hundred fifty (NT$250).
  大概二百五十元。

  > 核心句型 🎧 069-1
  > It will cost about
  > ＋ 金額.

- Here's your change—thirty five dollars (NT$35).
  這是找你的零錢三十五元。

- Maybe between five hundred (NT$500) to six hundred (NT$600).
  差不多五百元到六百元之間。

🎧 MP3 **070**

3. cost [kɔst] *v.* 花費（多少錢）
4. change [tʃendʒ] *n./v.* 〔不可數〕零錢；硬幣；更改

12 車資收費 B

D → **Driver**（司機）　　P → **Passenger**（乘客）　🎧 MP3 **071**

情境 ➊

D We've reached your destination. That will be four hundred sixty (NT$460).

我們已經抵達目的地了，總共是四百六十元。

P Can I **pay**[1] by credit card?

可以刷信用卡嗎？

D Sorry, **cash**[2] only.

不好意思，只收現金。

情境 ➋

P Do you accept credit cards?

你有收信用卡嗎？

D Yes, we do. You can **tap**[3]/**swipe**[4] your card right here.

有，可以。請在這邊感應卡片／刷卡。

P Perfect!

太好了！

D Thank you, have a great day.

謝謝，祝你有美好的一天。

 Word List

1. pay [pe] *v.* 支付；付款
2. cash [kæʃ] *n.* 現金
3. tap [tæp] *v.* 輕觸；點擊螢幕
4. swipe [swaɪp] *v.* 刷（卡）

★更多實用說法★　📻 MP3 **072**

司機

○ Okay, two hundred seventy-five (NT$275), please.
好。麻煩兩百七十五元。

○ I'm sorry. I don't have change.
不好意思，我沒有零錢找給你。

○ I'll get change in that 7-ELEVEN.
我去那家 7-ELEVEN 便利商店換錢。

○ The **fare**[6] is four hundred seventy (NT$470), but you only gave me three hundred seventy (NT$370).
車資是四百七十元，可是你只有給我三百七十元。

乘客

○ How much do I **owe**[5] you?
車資多少錢？

○ Thanks, here you go.
謝謝，來，錢給你。

○ Oh, I'm sorry. Here's the other hundred.
噢，抱歉。這邊是另一張一百元。

📻 MP3 **073**

5. owe [o] *v.* 該償還（錢）
6. fare [fɛr] *n.* 車資

13 下車

情境 ❶

D Here's my card **in case**[1] you need a taxi.

這是我的名片,如果你之後需要叫車可以找我。

> 核心句型 🎧 074-1
> Here's + 事物.

P Thanks! I will call you next time if I need a taxi.

謝啦!下次我需要叫車時,我會打給你。

D Be careful when opening the door. Watch behind you.

開門小心,注意後方來車。

情境 ❷

D There's too much traffic. Wait a second. Okay. It's safe to open the door.

現在車太多了,等一下喔,好,可以開車門了。

P **Oops**[2], I can't open the door.

哎呀,車門打不開耶。

D Let me **unlock**[3] the door.

我開一下門鎖。

 Word List

1. (just) in case 以防萬一
2. oops [ʊps] *int.* 語助詞,意思類似中文的「哎呀」,表達驚訝或後悔。
3. unlock [ʌnˋlɑk] *v.* 解鎖打開

★ 更多實用說法 ★　　🎧 MP3 **075**

乘客

● The door is locked.
車門鎖住了。

● Wait! I forgot my **umbrella**[4].
等一下！我忘記拿我的雨傘。

● Could you help me with my bags?
你能不能幫我拿一下我的行李？

司機

● Don't forget your personal **belongings**[5].
別忘記你的隨身物品。

● You dropped your **scarf**[6].
你圍巾掉了。

● Watch out for **motorcycles**[7] before getting out.
下車的時候注意後面的摩托車。

● Certainly! I'll get your **suitcase**[8] for you.
沒問題，我幫你拿行李下來。

🎧 MP3 **076**

4. umbrella [ʌmˈbrɛlə] *n.* 傘
5. belongings [bəˈlɔŋɪŋz] *n.*〔複數形〕攜帶物品

6. scarf [skɑrf] *n.* 圍巾；披巾
7. motorcycle [ˈmotəˌsaɪkl] *n.* 摩托車
8. suitcase [ˈsutˌkes] *n.* 手提箱

Ch 2

從叫車到下車

基本應對用語

☐ What's the basic fare?
跳錶起跳是多少錢？

☐ How much is the fare?
車資多少錢？

☐ How much does it cost to get to Yongkang Street?
到永康街要多少錢？

☐ Take a shortcut, please.
請走近一點的路線。

☐ Let's take the quickest route.
走最快的那條路吧。

☐ I'm a bit late. Can you drive faster?
我已經遲到了。你可以開快一點嗎？

☐ I think Xinsheng Elevated Road is faster.
我覺得走新生高架橋比較快。

☐ How long will it take to the station?
到車站要多久？

☐ How much farther is it?
還有多遠？

☐ This isn't the right place.
這不是我要去的地方。

MP3 **078**

☐ This is it. Thank you.
這邊就可以，謝謝。

☐ Here's fine. Thanks.
這邊就可以，謝謝。

☐ How much is it?
多少錢？

☐ Sorry, I don't have small bills.
我沒有小面額的紙鈔。

☐ Please pull over here, thanks.
前面請靠邊停車，謝謝。

☐ Can you give me a receipt?
能給我一張收據嗎？

☐ Here is one hundred fifty dollars (NT$150).
這邊是一百五十元。

☐ Keep the change.
零錢不用找了。

☐ This isn't the right change.
找的零錢數目不對。

☐ That would be great!
（如果那樣）就太好了！

基本應對用語

☐ The basic fare is eighty-five dollars (NT$85).
車資起跳是八十五元。

☐ About thirty minutes. Are you in a hurry?
大概三十分鐘左右。你趕時間嗎？

☐ I'll follow the GPS. Is that okay?
我就跟著導航走，可以嗎？

☐ Is that okay with you?
這樣可以嗎？

☐ I know a few shortcuts, but it depends on traffic.
我知道一些捷徑，但是也要看交通狀況。

☐ It's hard to say.
很難說喔。

☐ I'll get you there as quickly as possible.
我會盡快載你到達目的地。

☐ Is this the place?
是這個地方嗎？

☐ Alright! Here we are!
我們到囉！

☐ That will be six hundred twenty five dollars (NT$625).
總共是六百二十五元。

☐ Three hundred fifty (350), please.
（車資）三百五十元，謝謝。

🎧 MP3 **080**

☐ Here is the station. Three hundred eighty dollars (NT$380), please.

車站到了。總共是三百八十元。

☐ Do you have smaller bills?

有面額小一點的鈔票嗎？

☐ Do you need a receipt?

你有需要收據嗎？

☐ Let me turn on the light.

讓我開一下燈。

☐ Don't worry!

別擔心！

☐ Be careful!

小心！

☐ Let me help you with that.

我幫你。

☐ Don't forget your personal belongings.

別忘記你的隨身物品。

☐ Thank you very much.

非常感謝。

☐ Have a good one!

祝你愉快。

☐ You're welcome.

不客氣。

Notes

Chapter 3

萬用聊天話題

Part 1

台灣美食

D → **Driver**（司機）　　P → **Passenger**（乘客）　🎧 MP3 **081**

情境 ❶

D Have you tried bubble milk tea?
你有喝過珍珠奶茶嗎？

> 核心句型 🎧 081-1
> Have you tried ＋ 食物？

P No, any **recommendations**[1]?
沒喝過，有推薦的嗎？

D My **favorite**[2] is KEBUKE.
我最喜歡可不可熟成紅茶。

情境 ❷

D By the way, do you like bubble milk tea?
對了，你喜歡珍珠奶茶嗎？

> 核心句型 🎧 081-2
> Do you like ＋ 食物？

P Yeah, I really enjoy it.
嗯，我很喜歡。

D Me too! It's perfect for sunny days.
我也是！夏天最適合喝珍奶了。

 Word List

1. recommendation [ˌrɛkəmɛnˈdeʃən] *n.* 推薦
2. favorite [ˈfevərɪt] *n./adj.* 最喜歡的人或物；最喜歡的

★更多實用說法★ 🎧 MP3 **082**

司機

● If you love muscovado sugar, you can try Tiger Sugar.
如果你愛黑糖，你可以試試老虎堂。

● If you like tea latte, then it's Milksha.
如果你喜歡茶拿鐵，那就是迷客夏了。

● If you prefer fruit tea, you can try DaYung's Tea.
如果你偏好水果茶，那你可以試試大苑子。

● If you are a fan of Taiwanese tea, Ten Ren Tea is a must-try.
如果你喜歡台灣茶葉，你一定要試試看天仁茗茶。

● I highly recommend Guiji. It's very **special**[3].
我超推薦龜記，很特別。

● Wushiland Boba is one of the oldest chain stores.
五十嵐是台灣最老的飲料連鎖店之一。

● It's **sweet**[4] and **chewy**[5].
這個甜甜的、QQ 的。

● It's very **delicious**[6]!
這非常好吃！

🎧 MP3 **083**

---

3. special [ˈspɛʃəl] *adj.* 特別的

4. sweet [swit] *adj.* 甜的

5. chewy [ˈtʃuɪ] *adj.* 有嚼勁的

6. delicious [dɪˈlɪʃəs] *adj.* 美味的

D → **Driver**（司機）　　P → **Passenger**（乘客）　　🚗 MP3 **084**

情境 ❶

P I'm just **exploring**¹ the **city**². Any recommendations?
我想探索這個城市。有什麼推薦嗎？

D You've got to try Din Tai Fung. Its xiaolongbao is a must-eat.
你一定要試試鼎泰豐，小籠包是必吃的一道菜。

P That **sounds**³ great. What's the place called again?
聽起來很棒，你剛剛說那家餐廳叫什麼？

D It's called Din Tai Fung. There's one in Taipei 101.
叫作鼎泰豐，台北 101 裡就有一家。

> 核心句型 🚗 084-1
> It's called + 名字.

情境 ❷

D Have you tried Taiwanese soup dumpling?
你有吃過台灣的湯包嗎？

P Yes, I have tried Din Tai Fung. I love xiaolongbao so much!
有，我吃過鼎泰豐，我很喜歡小籠包！

D You also can try Dian Shui Lou. That's my favorite.
你也可以試試點水樓，我最喜歡他們的湯包。

> 核心句型 🚗 084-2
> You can try + 事物.

P **Awesome**⁴! Thanks for the recommendation.
太好了！謝謝你的推薦。

 Word List

1. **explore** [ɪk'splor] v. 探索
2. **city** ['sɪtɪ] n. 城市

3. **sound** [saʊnd] v. 聽起來
4. **awesome** ['ɔsəm] adj. 很讚的

★ 更多實用說法 ★   🎧 MP3 **085**

司機

- The **restaurant**[5] is top-notch.
  那家餐廳超棒。

- It's **famous**[6] not only in Taiwan but around the world.
  它不只是在台灣有名，全世界都有名。

- Trust me! You will love it!
  相信我！你會喜歡的！

- I recommend xiaolongbao—Taiwanese **dumplings**[7]!
  我推薦小籠包——台灣的餃子！

- The skin is thin and the meat inside is **juicy**[8].
  皮薄而內餡多汁。

- They have an open kitchen. It's very cool.
  他們有開放廚房，很酷！

- I love their chocolate xiaolongbao. It's very special.
  我喜歡他們的巧克力小籠包，非常特別。

🎧 MP3 **086**

5. restaurant [ˈrɛstərənt] *n.* 餐廳
6. famous [ˈfeməs] *adj.* 著名的
7. dumpling [ˈdʌmplɪŋ] *n.* 餃子
8. juicy [ˈdʒusɪ] *adj.* 多汁的

03 鹹酥雞

D → **Driver**（司機）　P → **Passenger**（乘客）　MP3 **087**

情境 ❶

D Have you tried Taiwanese popcorn **chicken**[1]? It's a must-eat!

你有吃過台灣鹹酥雞嗎？那是必吃的喔！

P Where can I get it?

去那裡吃？

D There are so many. My favorite is in Shida Night Market.

有很多家都很好吃，不過我最喜歡的是師大夜市裡面那一家。

P Wait, is it called Shiyun Fried Chicken?

等一下，你說的那家是不是叫作師園鹹酥雞？

D Yes! 沒錯！

情境 ❷

D Deep-fried chicken **fillet**[2] is a must-try. Have you tried it?

炸雞排是必吃的，你有吃過嗎？

P What's so special about it?

特別在哪裡？

D It's like the king of street food.

炸雞排就像台灣小吃之王一樣。

🔋 Word List

1. chicken [ˈtʃɪkɪn] *n.* 雞肉
2. fillet [ˈfɪlɪt] *n.* 肉排；魚排

★更多實用說法★　🎧 MP3 **088**

司機

● Popcorn chicken is a must-try!
鹹酥雞絕對是必吃的！

● It's very **yummy**[3]!
真的非常好吃！

● It's a great late-night **snack**[4].
它是很棒的宵夜。

● **Crispy**[5] on the outside, **tender**[6] on the inside.
外酥內嫩。

● It's similar to American popcorn chicken.
很像美式雞米花！

● I love deep-fried chicken fillet more.
我更喜歡雞排。

核心句型 🎧 088-1

I love + 某物 + more.

● Don't leave Taiwan without trying it.
離開台灣之前一定要嚐一嚐。

● You're gonna love it!
你會愛上它的！

🎧 MP3 **089**

3. yummy [ˈjʌmɪ] *adj.* 美味的
4. snack [snæk] *n.* 點心；小吃

5. crispy [ˈkrɪspɪ] *adj.* 酥脆的
6. tender [ˈtɛndə] *adj.* 嫩的

Ⓓ → **Driver**（司機）　Ⓟ → **Passenger**（乘客）　🎧 MP3 **090**

情境 ❶

Ⓟ I'm looking for a **classic**[1] Taiwanese **breakfast**[2].
Any recommendations?

我想找正統的台灣早餐，你有什麼建議嗎？

Ⓓ You've got to try soy milk and youtiao.

那你一定要試試豆漿跟油條。

Ⓟ What's that?

那是什麼呀？

Ⓓ It's a breakfast combo. It's very popular in Taiwan.

那是一種在台灣很受歡迎的早餐組合。

Ⓟ **Interesting**[3]! Where can I get this?

好有趣！我在哪裡可以吃到？

Ⓓ You can have a nice Taiwanese breakfast at Yong He Dou Jiang.

你可以在永和豆漿吃到美味的台式早餐。

情境 ❷

Ⓓ Do you like Taiwanese breakfast?

你喜歡台式早餐嗎？

Ⓟ Oh, yes! I love danbing.

噢，喜歡啊！我愛蛋餅。

Ⓓ I like danbing, too.

我也喜歡蛋餅。

★ 更多實用說法 ★　☎ MP3 **091**

司機

- Some people say it's Chinese omelet.
  有人說這是中式煎蛋捲。

- Chinese fried dough is **tasty**[4].
  油條很好吃。

- Crispy on the outside, **fluffy**[5] on the inside.
  外面酥脆，裡面鬆軟。

- You can **dip**[6] youtiao in soy milk.
  油條可以蘸著豆漿一起吃。

- Don't forget to try 'shaobing youtiao.'
  別忘了吃燒餅油條。

 Word List　　　　　　　　　　　　　☎ MP3 **092**

1. classic [ˈklæsɪk] *adj.* 經典的；一流的
2. breakfast [ˈbrɛkfəst] *n.* 早餐
3. interesting [ˈɪntərɪstɪŋ] *adj.* 有趣的
4. tasty [ˈtestɪ] *adj.* 美味的
5. fluffy [ˈflʌfɪ] *adj.* 鬆軟的；蓬鬆的
6. dip [dɪp] *v.* 浸；蘸

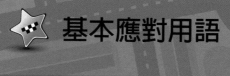

基本應對用語

☐ Bubble tea is my comfort food.
珍珠奶茶是我最愛的療癒系食物。

☐ Sesame flatbread is <u>my favorite</u>.
燒餅是我的最愛。

核心句型 🛞 093-1
_____ is my favorite.

☐ It just melts in your mouth.
這入口即化。

☐ It's so good.
這很好吃。

☐ It's mouthwatering.
這很美味。（讓人口水直流）

☐ It's very tasty.
這很美味。

☐ I recommend Fuhang Soy Milk.
我推薦阜杭豆漿。

☐ (Have you) Ever tried the food around here?
你有吃過附近的美食嗎？

☐ It's a must-try/must-eat/must-buy.
這是必吃 / 必買。

☐ Taiwan is a foodie's paradise。
台灣是美食愛好者的天堂。

☐ If you like food, you're at the right place.
如果你喜歡美食，你來對地方了。

D → **Driver**（司機）　　P → **Passenger**（乘客）　　🎧 MP3 **094**

D My favorite snack is popcorn chicken.
鹹酥雞是我的最愛。

P Same here!
我也是耶！

D Shuijianbao is my all-time favorite.
水煎包是我的最愛。

P Oh, you're speaking my language!
噢，你說的沒錯！（我也是這樣覺得）

D It's so good.
這個好好吃喔。

P I know, right? It's so delicious!
對啊，這個真的很好吃！

D It's mouthwatering.
這讓人食指大動耶。

P Totally! The thought of it is making my mouth water already.
沒錯！光用想的就讓我口水直流了。

D I recommend Gua bao, the Taiwanese hamburger.
我推薦刈包，那是台灣的漢堡。

P Great! I'll make sure to try it.
太好了！我一定會去吃吃看。

D Ever tried the food around here?

你有吃過附近的美食嗎？

P Oh, absolutely! The local food is fantastic.

噢，當然有啊！這邊的食物很好吃。

D It's a must-eat.

這是必吃的喔。

P Got it! Thanks.

我知道了，謝啦！

D If you're a foodie, you've come to the right place.

如果你喜歡美食，你來對地方了。

P That's why I feel right at home here.

這就是為什麼我在這裡感到如此親切呢。

D Taiwan is a foodie's paradise.

台灣是美食愛好者的天堂。

P It sure is.

的確如此。

★ 熱門台式早餐補充 ★

燒餅	Shaobing / sesame flatbread
油條	Youtiao / Chinese fried dough / fried bread stick
飯糰	Fantuan / sticky rice ball
蛋餅	Danbing / Chinese omelet
饅頭	Mantou / steamed bun
水煎包	Shuijianbao / pan-fried bun
小籠包	Xiaolongbao / soup dumpling
蘿蔔糕	Luobogao / Chinese radish cake

Part 2

雙北著名景點

01　台北 101

D → Driver（司機）　　P → Passenger（乘客）　　🎧 MP3 **095**

情境 ❶

P What's a must-visit place around here?

這邊附近必去的景點是什麼？

D Taipei 101 is a must-see. It used to be the tallest building in the world.

台北 101 一定要去！它之前還是世界第一高樓呢。

P How much is the **ticket**[1]?

門票多少錢？

D It's four hundred twenty dollars. It's worth it!

門票是四百二十元。值得去喔！

情境 ❷

P Any must-visit spots around here?

這裡附近有什麼必去的景點嗎？

D I recommend the National Palace Museum. It has many **historical**[2] **treasures**[3].

我推薦故宮，那邊有非常多珍貴的歷史文物。

P Nice! Where can I enjoy Taipei's night view?

謝謝。那有哪些地方我可以看台北夜景呢？

D Oh, you can go to Taipei 101. The view from there is **amazing**[4].

噢，你可以去台北 101，那裡的夜景真的超棒！

★更多實用說法★　🔊 MP3 **096**

司機

- Taipei 101 Observatory is a good place to watch the sunset.
  台北 101 觀景台是個看夕陽的好地方。

- The Observatory ticket office is on the 5th floor.
  觀景台的售票口在五樓。

- It's worth every penny.
  你花的錢絕對值得。

- It's a famous **skyscraper**[5].
  它是有名的摩天大樓。

- Enjoy the night view of Taipei.
  好好享受台北的夜景。

  > 核心句型 🔊 096-1
  > Enjoy + 事物.

- Besides the view, there are cool **shops**[6] and restaurants.
  除了夜景之外,你還可以逛很多小店跟餐廳。

 Word List　🔊 MP3 **097**

1. ticket [ˈtɪkɪt] *n.* 入場券;車票
2. historical [hɪsˈtɔrɪkl̩] *adj.* 歷史的
3. treasure [ˈtrɛʒɚ] *n.* 寶物
4. amazing [əˈmezɪŋ] *adj.* 極好的
5. skyscraper [ˈskaɪˌskrepɚ] *n.* 摩天大樓
6. shop [ʃɑp] *n.* 商店

Ⓓ → **Driver**（司機）　　Ⓟ → **Passenger**（乘客）　🎧 MP3 **098**

情境 ❶

Ⓟ Any interesting spots around Xinyi **District**¹?

信義區附近有沒有什麼有趣的景點值得去看看呢？

Ⓓ It's a great place to go shopping. There are many department stores. You also can go to VIESHOW **Cinemas**². You can catch the **latest**³ **films**⁴.

那邊是很好購物的地方，有很多百貨公司。你還可以去威秀影城，看最新上映的電影。

情境 ❷

Ⓟ I want to pick up some snacks for friends and family. Any recommendations?

我想買點好吃的回去給親朋好友，你有什麼推薦的嗎？

Ⓓ The **basement**⁵ floor of the department stores, they have really good **pastries**⁶, like pineapple cakes and mung bean pastry.

你可以去百貨公司 B1，那邊有很多好吃的點心，像是鳳梨酥或綠豆碰。

Ⓟ Are they Taiwanese **traditional**⁷ pastries?

那些是台灣傳統點心嗎？

Ⓓ Yes, they're very tasty and special.

對，他們很好吃又很特別。

★更多實用說法★　🔊 MP3 **099**

司機

◉ Xinyi District is like the Manhattan of Taipei.
信義區就像是台北的曼哈頓。

◉ It's a famous shopping district.
這是一個著名的購物商圈。

◉ This place is perfect for shopping.
這個地方非常適合購物。

◉ It's a great place to buy **gifts**[8] for friends and family.
這是一個可以幫朋友和家人挑選小禮物的好地方。

◉ It's famous for **high-end**[9] malls and **fancy**[10] restaurants.
這裡以高檔購物中心和精緻餐廳而聞名。

◉ The place is always buzzing with energy.
這個地方總是充滿活力。

 Word List　🔊 MP3 **100**

1. district [ˈdɪstrɪkt] *n.* 區
2. cinema [ˈsɪnəmə] *n.* 電影院
3. latest [ˈletɪst] *adj.* 最新的
4. film [fɪlm] *n./v.* （拍攝）電影
5. basement [ˈbesmənt] *n.* 地下室
6. pastry [ˈpestrɪ] *n.* 油酥糕點；茶點
7. traditional [trəˈdɪʃənl] *adj.* 傳統的
8. gift [gɪft] *n.* 禮物
9. high-end [ˈhaɪˌɛnd] *adj.* 高檔的
10. fancy [ˈfænsɪ] *adj.* 豪華的；昂貴的

D → **Driver**（司機） P → **Passenger**（乘客） MP3 **101**

情境 ❶

P What are your **go-to**[1] places for hiking?
哪些地方是郊外走走的首選地點？

D Have you been to Yangmingshan?
你有去過陽明山嗎？

> 核心句型 101-1
> Have you been to + 地點？

P No, but I heard it's got some great night views.
沒有，但我聽說山上的夜景很棒。

D Yes, there are many restaurants with good food and amazing night views.
對啊，山上有很多餐廳，你可以邊吃美食邊欣賞夜景。

情境 ❷

P Any places worth checking out?
有什麼推薦值得去看看的地方嗎？

D I recommend Yangmingshan.
我推薦你去陽明山走走。

P Oh, my friend said that there's a circular **trail**[2] in Qingtiangang Grassland.
噢，我朋友說那邊有個環形步道在擎天岡。

D Yes, that's right! Actually, there are many trails. You can get **information**[3] at Qingtiangang Visitor Center.
沒錯！其實，山上有許多路線，你可以去擎天岡遊客中心詢問相關資訊。

 ☎ MP3 **102**

司機

- Yangmingshan National Park is worth visiting.
  陽明山國家公園值得一遊。

- The flowers are in full bloom. It's very beautiful.
  花朵盛開，景色非常美麗。

- March is the best time to see cherry blossoms.
  三月是賞櫻花的最佳時機。

- The flower **festival**[4] has been held for more than sixty years.
  陽明山花季已經舉辦了六十多年。

- On weekends and holidays, there is traffic control.
  週末和假日會實施交通管制。

- You can take **shuttle**[5] buses. It's very **convenient**[6].
  你可以搭乘接駁車，非常方便。

- In winter, you can enjoy hot springs up there.
  在冬天，你還可以在陽明山泡溫泉。

Ch 3
萬用聊天話題

Word List ☎ MP3 **103**

1. **go-to** [ˈgoˌtu] *adj.* （為做某件事情的）必找的（人）；必去的（地方）
2. **trail** [trel] *n.* 小徑；小道
3. **information** [ˌɪnfəˈmeʃən] *n.* 資訊；消息
4. **festival** [ˈfɛstəvl] *n.* 節日
5. **shuttle** [ˈʃʌtl] *n.* 接駁車
6. **convenient** [kənˈvinjənt] *adj.* 方便的

04 寺廟

情境 ❶

P What's that?

那是什麼？

D It's Longshan Temple. It's almost three hundred years old.

那是龍山寺，是一座近三百年的寺廟。

P Wow, it's a historical building.

哇，是歷史建築呢。

D Yes, we call it Longshansi. 'Si' means temple.

是啊，我們說龍山寺，「寺」就是廟的意思。

情境 ❷

P Can you recommend some must-see **attractions**[1] nearby?

你可以推薦一下附近一定要去逛逛的地方嗎？

D Xiahai City God Temple is worth visiting.

霞海城隍廟很值得去看看。

P Where's that temple?

在哪裡？

D In Dadaocheng. You can also enjoy the old streets. And there are lots of **local**[2] snacks.

就在大稻埕。你還可以漫步老街，而且有很多道地小吃。

★更多實用說法★ 😑 MP3 **105**

司機

- In Taiwan, we say 'bai bai.'
  在台灣，我們說「拜拜」。

- We put two hands together and **pray**[3] to our Gods.
  我們合掌，向我們的神明祈福。

- Yue Lao is the god of **marriage**[4] and love.
  月老是掌管姻緣的神明。

- The birthday of Mazu is a huge **celebration**[5].
  媽祖的生日是一個盛大的慶典。

- In Chinese, eight is **lucky**[6] because it means getting rich.
  在中文裡，數字 8 是吉利的，因為它的意思是發財。

- In Chinese, four is **unlucky**[6] because it sounds like death.
  在中文裡，數字 4 是不吉利的，因為它的發音聽起來跟「死」很像。

 Word List 😑 MP3 **106**

1. attraction [əˋtrækʃən] *n.*（旅遊）景點
2. local [ˋlokl] *adj.* 當地的；本地的
3. pray [pre] *v.* 祈禱
4. marriage [ˋmærɪdʒ] *n.* 婚姻
5. celebration [ˌsɛləˋbreʃən] *n.* 慶祝
6. (un)lucky [(ʌn)ˋlʌkɪ] *adj.*（不）幸運的

05 夜市

D → **Driver**（司機）　P → **Passenger**（乘客）　 MP3 **107**

情境 ❶

P What are the places I should definitely **check out**[1]?

有哪些地方是你覺得一定要去看看的？

D Have you been to Shilin Night Market?

你有去過士林夜市了嗎？

P No, do you recommend it?

沒有耶，你推薦嗎？

D Yeah, it's the biggest one in Taipei. You can try all kinds of street food.

對啊，士林夜市是台北市規模最大的，你可以嘗試各種路邊攤小吃。

情境 ❷

P How about Raohe Night Market? Is it good?

那饒河街夜市呢？好玩嗎？

D Raohe Night Market is famous, too.

饒河街夜市也很有名啊。

P How about Keelung Night Market?

那基隆夜市呢？

D That's in Keelung City. You can go there by train, bus, or taxi.

那個夜市在基隆市。去基隆，你可以搭火車、公車或計程車。

★更多實用說法★ MP3 **108**

司機

◉ Night markets in Taiwan are like food **carnivals**².
台灣的夜市就像美食嘉年華。

◉ It's a **foodie's**³ paradise.
這是美食愛好者的天堂。

◉ Taiwan is famous for its street food.
台灣以街頭小吃而聞名。

◉ There are many trendy shops.
有很多時興的小商店。

◉ Go to night markets for a real Taiwan **experience**⁴.
去夜市體驗一下道地台灣生活。

◉ Enjoy the special **vibes**⁵.
感受這特別的氛圍。

 Word List MP3 **109**

1. check out【口語】試試；看看
2. carnival [`kɑrnəvl] *n.* 嘉年華會
3. foodie [fudɪ] *n.*【俚語】美食家
4. experience [ɪk`spɪrɪəns] *n.* 經驗；體驗
5. vibes [vaɪbz] *n.*〔複數形〕氣氛；感覺

06 西門町 / 淡水 / 貓空纜車

⊡ → **Driver**（司機）　⊡ → **Passenger**（乘客）　🎧 MP3 **110**

情境 ❶

⊡ To Ximending, please.
到西門町，麻煩你。

⊡ No problem. There's a famous historical building, have you been there?
沒問題。那邊有一個有名的歷史建築，你有去過嗎？

⊡ No, it's my first time.
沒有，這是我第一次去西門町。

> 核心句型 🎧 110-1
> It used to be + 事物.

⊡ It's called The Red House. It used to be a **theater**¹.
叫作紅樓，曾經是戲院。

情境 ❷

⊡ Do you know where to catch the best sunset in Taipei?
你知道在台北哪裡可以看夕陽嗎？

⊡ You can enjoy the beautiful sunset in Tamsui. You can also ride a **bike**² there.
你可以在淡水欣賞美麗的日落。你也可以在那裡騎自行車。

 Word List

1. **theater** [ˋθɪətə] *n.* 劇場；電影院
2. **bike** [baɪk] *n.* 自行車

★ 更多實用說法 ★　🎧 MP3 **111**

司機

● Have you been to The Red House in Ximending?
你有去過西門町的紅樓嗎？

● You can **take the ferry**[3] from Tamsui to Bali.
你可以從淡水搭渡輪到八里。

● You can take a short walk along the **river**[4].
你可以沿著河邊散步。

● Don't miss Fort Santo Domingo and the old street in Tamsui.
別錯過淡水紅毛城和老街。

● Take the **gondola**[5] to Maokong. There are many tea houses.
搭乘纜車上貓空，那邊有很多茶坊。

● Don't forget to try some tea **cuisine**[6].
別忘了嚐嚐看茶葉做的料理。

> 核心句型 🎧 111-1
> Don't forget to try + 食物.

Ch 3

萬用聊天話題

🎧 MP3 **112**

---

3. ferry [ˈfɛrɪ] *n.* 渡輪

4. river [ˈrɪvɚ] *n.* 河

5. gondola [ˈgɑndələ] *n.* 纜車

6. cuisine [kwɪˈzin] *n.* 料理

D → **Driver**（司機）　　P → **Passenger**（乘客）　　🎧 MP3 **113**

情境 ❶

P The National Palace Museum, is it worth **visiting**[1]?

故宮博物院，值得一去嗎？

D Of course! Are you into **history**[2]?

當然啊！你對歷史感興趣嗎？

> 核心句型 🎧 113-1
> Are you into + 事物？

P Yeah, I love history.

是的，我喜歡歷史。

D Then you'll enjoy it. Don't forget to see the most famous **cabbage**[3] in the world.

那你一定會喜歡故宮博物院的。別忘了看看世界上最有名的「白菜」。

P I know, I heard that people line up just to get to see that.

我知道，我聽說看那些古物都要排隊呢。

情境 ❷

> 核心句型 🎧 113-2
> How was ...?

D How was the National Palace Museum? Did you find it **enjoyable**[4]?

故宮博物院怎麼樣？你覺得好玩嗎？

P It was amazing! So much history in one place.

太棒了！這麼豐富的歷史集中在一個地方。

D Glad you liked it! What was your favorite?

很高興你喜歡！你最喜歡的是什麼？

P The **Jadeite**[5] Cabbage and the Meat-shaped **Stone**[6] are amazing.

翠玉白菜和肉形石讓我印象深刻。

★更多實用說法★　 MP3 **114**

司機

● It's the largest museum in Taiwan.
這是台灣最大的博物館。

● It's a **world-class**[7] museum.
是世界一流的博物館。

● The museum hosts exhibitions every year.
故宮博物院每年都舉辦展覽。

● Don't miss the Jadeite Cabbage and the Meat-shaped Stone.
別錯過翠玉白菜和肉形石。

● They're the 'rock stars' of the museum.
它們是故宮的巨星。

 Word List　　　　　　　　　　 MP3 **115**

1. visit [`vɪzɪt] *v./n.* 參觀；拜訪
2. history [`hɪstərɪ] *n.* 歷史
3. cabbage [`kæbɪdʒ] *n.* 白菜；捲心菜
4. enjoyable [ɪn`dʒɔɪəbl] *adj.* 有樂趣的

5. jadeite [`dʒedaɪt] *n.* 玉；翡翠
6. stone [ston] *n.* 石頭
7. world-class [`wɝld.klæs] *adj.* 世界級的

08 九份 / 金瓜石

情境 ❶

P I heard a lot about Jiufen, the **mountain**[1] **town**[2]. Is it worth a visit?

我聽很多人說到九份這個山城，值得一去嗎？

D Sure! You will love the old streets, tea houses, and beautiful views.

當然！你會愛上老街、老茶館和美麗的風景。

P Great! What else? Any interesting history?

太棒了！還有呢？有沒有什麼有趣的歷史？

D Yeah, Jiufen used to be a gold **mining**[3] town.

有啊，九份以前是個挖金礦的山城。

P Hey, isn't this the place where they filmed 'A City of Sadness'?

嘿，這是不是《悲情城市》拍攝的地方？

D Yes, you're right!

沒錯，你說對了！

情境 ❷

D The Gold Ecological Park in Jinguashi is a must-visit.

金瓜石的黃金博物館是一個必訪的地方。

P Sounds interesting.

聽起來很有趣。

D And it's not just a park. There's a museum, too.

而且這不僅是一個公園而已，還有一個博物館。

★ 更多實用說法 ★　🎧 MP3 **117**

司機

● Jiufen is a small **village**[4] in the mountains.
九份是一個位於山區的小村莊。

● You can walk into the old tunnels.
你可以走進古老的礦坑隧道。

● The old streets are **charming**[5].
老街很迷人。

● The film 'A City of Sadness' was shot in Jiufen.
電影《悲情城市》就是在九份取景的。

● Jiufen is famous for **taro**[6] balls.
九份芋圓最出名了。

● Don't forget to try Taiwanese tea in Jiufen.
記得去九份品嚐台灣茶。

 Word List　🎧 MP3 **118**

1. **mountain** ['mauntn] *n.* 山

2. **town** [taun] *n.* 小鎮

3. **mining** ['maɪnɪŋ] *n.* 採礦

4. **village** ['vɪlɪdʒ] *n.* 村莊

5. **charming** ['tʃɑrmɪŋ] *adj.* 有魅力的

6. **taro** ['taro] *n.* 芋頭

Ch 3
萬用聊天話題

基本應對用語

🎧 MP3 **119**

☐ Hey there! Welcome to Taipei/Taichung/Tainan/Kaohsiung.
嗨！歡迎來到台北 / 台中 / 台南 / 高雄。

☐ How do you like Taoyuan/Hsinchu/Miaoli/Yilan?
你喜歡桃園 / 新竹 / 苗栗 / 宜蘭嗎？

☐ The breathtaking view! Don't miss out.
美到令人屏息的景色，千萬別錯過！

☐ If you're into history/hiking, you'll love this place.
如果你喜歡歷史 / 健行，你會喜歡這個地方的。

☐ If you're a fan of art, I recommend the Museum of Contemporary Art.
如果你喜歡藝術，我推薦你去當代藝術館。

☐ It's a hidden gem.
這是隱藏版（美食 / 秘境）。

☐ It's very popular.
這很受歡迎。

☐ You will like/love it.
你會喜歡的。

☐ I hope you like it.
我希望你會喜歡。

☐ Have a great time in Taipei!
祝你在台北玩得愉快！

D → **Driver**（司機）　P → **Passenger**（乘客）　🎧 MP3 **120**

D Hey there! Welcome to Chiayi.

哈囉！歡迎來到嘉義。

P Thank you. I'm excited to explore the city.

謝謝你，我迫不及待要探索這個城市。

D How do you like Hualien?

你覺得花蓮怎麼樣？

P I'm loving Hualien! The city has a great vibe and so much to see.

我喜歡花蓮！這座城市充滿活力，還有很多好玩的地方。

D The amazing night view! Don't miss out.

夜景很棒，千萬別錯過！

P I won't!

我不會錯過的！

D If you're into the sea, you'll love this place.

如果你喜歡海，你一定會喜歡這個地方。

P Oh, I am! I can't wait.

噢，我喜歡海啊！我等不及去看看了。

D It's a hidden gem.

這個地方很少人知道，是隱藏版的喔！

P Really? I can't wait to explore it.

真的嗎？我迫不及待要去探索了。

D It's very popular.

這很受歡迎。

P Oh, that's good to know!

噢，那太好了！

D You will love it.

你會喜歡的。

P I'm sure I will. Thanks for the recommendation.

我相信我會喜歡的，謝謝推薦。

★ 熱門夜市小吃補充 ★

蚵仔煎	Oyster Omelet
臭豆腐	Stinky Tofu
刈包	Gua Bao / Taiwanese hamburger
滷肉飯	Lu Rou Fan / braised pork over rice
肉圓	Ba Wan / Taiwanese meatball
胡椒餅	Black Pepper Bun

Part 3

台灣文化・特色

01 天氣

情境 ❶

D Are you just visiting?
你是來旅遊嗎？

P No, I'm here on business.
不是，我是來出差的。

D It's really **humid**[1] today, right?
今天很濕熱，對不對？

P Totally! Is it usually like this?
對啊！通常都這樣嗎？

情境 ❷

D The **weather**[2] is nice today, not too hot.
今天天氣很好，不會太熱。

P I know. It's sunny and clear.
就是說啊，陽光普照、晴空萬里。

D The weather is perfect for a short walk.
這個天氣很適合到處走走。

P That's right.
沒錯。

★更多實用說法★　🎧 MP3 **122**

司機

● It's a beautiful day, isn't it?
今天是個美好的一天，不是嗎？

● Summer in Taiwan is like outdoor sauna.
台灣的夏天就像戶外三溫暖。

● The moon is out tonight.
今天晚上月亮出來了。

● A **typhoon**[4] is coming this **weekend**[5]. Be careful!
這個週末可能會有颱風。要小心！

● It looks like it might rain.
看起來好像快下雨了。

● The weather is **terrible**[6], isn't it?
天氣真不好，不是嗎？

● The air feels so fresh after the rain.
雨後的空氣很清新。

 Word List　🎧 MP3 **123**

1. humid [ˋhjumɪd] *adj.* 潮濕的
2. weather [ˋwɛðɚ] *n.* 天氣
3. mild [maɪld] *adj.* 溫和的；暖和的
4. typhoon [taɪˋfun] *n.* 颱風
5. weekend [ˋwikˋɛnd] *n.* 週末
6. terrible [ˋtɛrəbl] *adj.* 糟糕的；嚴重的

物價／時事

情境 ❶

Ⓓ Many things are **pricier**[1]. Did you notice that?

很多東西變貴了，你有發現嗎？

Ⓟ Yeah! Street food's my go-to, but **prices**[2] have gone up. What's your take?

對啊！我平常都吃小吃，但價格漲了不少。你覺得呢？

Ⓓ I don't know, after the COVID-19, and then **inflation**[3] ...

我也不太確定，可能是因為 COVID-19，再加上通膨的原因吧。

情境 ❷

Ⓟ I love the energy of live **performances**[4]. How about you?

我很喜歡現場演出的那種感覺。你呢？

Ⓓ Same here. Coldplay went to Kaohsiung, right? I was there!

我也是。Coldplay 去了高雄，對吧？我有去！

Ⓟ How nice! Billie Eilish was supposed to come to Taiwan, you know, but it got **canceled**[5] because of COVID-19. I had already got the tickets, so sad.

太讚了吧！Billie Eilish 本來要來台灣，你知道嗎？但因為 COVID-19 取消了。我都買到票了，真的很可惜。

★ 更多實用說法 ★　🎧 MP3 **125**

司機

核心句型 🎧 125-1
I used to ..., but now ...

● I used to buy Starbucks every day, but now I make **instant**[6] coffee.
我之前每天都買一杯星巴克，但現在我改喝即溶咖啡了。

● I used to dine out, but now I cook at home every night.
我以前都外食，但現在我每天晚上都在家裡煮。

● Prices are going up.
物價一直在上漲。

● Everything is getting more **expensive**[7].
現在所有東西都變貴了。

● It feels like the **economy**[8] is getting better.
感覺經濟好像正在好轉。

🅿️ Word List　🎧 MP3 **126**

1. pricey [`praɪsi] *adj.* 價格高的
2. price [praɪs] *n.* 價格
3. inflation [ɪn`fleʃən] *n.* 通貨膨脹
4. performance [pɚ`fɔrməns] *n.* 表演
5. cancel [`kænsl] *v.* 取消；終止
6. instant [`ɪnstənt] *adj.* 即刻的；立即的
7. expensive [ɪk`spɛnsɪv] *adj.* 昂貴的
8. economy [ɪ`kɑnəmɪ] *n.* 經濟

Ch 3

萬用聊天話題

情境 ❶

D Taipei Main Station is a **transportation**[1] **hub**[2]. Trains, High Speed Rail, and MRT all in one.

台北車站是一個交通樞紐。火車、高鐵和捷運一應俱全。

P That's **fantastic**[3]! And I heard there's a food court.

太棒了！而且我聽說那裡還有美食街。

D Yes, that's correct! Right inside the station.

是的，沒錯！就在車站裡面。

情境 ❷

P My kid told me yesterday that he doesn't want to get a job in the future; he wants to be a YouTuber. I'm going crazy.

昨天我兒子告訴我，他將來不想找工作，他想當 YouTuber。我要瘋了。

D Wow, how old is your kid?

哇，你兒子多大了？

P He's in the first year of junior high. I work so hard to earn money, and he tells me he wants to be a YouTuber. I'm speechless.

他國一。我辛苦賺錢，他告訴我他想當 YouTuber，我真的無言。

D He's still young. It's hard to say what the future holds.

他還很年輕，很難說未來到底會發生什麼事啊。

★ 更多實用說法 ★　🎧 MP3 **128**

司機

● They have all kinds of Taiwanese **goodies**[4].
他們有各種各樣的台灣美食。

● The High Speed Rail is the fastest way to **travel**[5] in Taiwan.
高鐵是台灣城市之間最快的交通方式。

● The THSR stations have signs in English.
高鐵車站的標示有英文。

● It's tourist-friendly.
對遊客相當友善。

● Do you follow any influencers or YouTubers?
你有關注哪些網紅或 YouTuber 嗎？

● TikTok is my go-to for funny videos.
抖音是我看好笑影片的首選。

 Word List　🎧 MP3 **129**

1. transportation [ˌtrænspəˈteʃən] *n.* 交通
2. hub [hʌb] *n.* 中心
3. fantastic [fænˈtæstɪk] *adj.* 極好的
4. goody [ˈgudɪ] *n.* 好東西（尤指食物）
5. travel [ˈtrævl] *v.* 旅行

D → **Driver**（司機）　P → **Passenger**（乘客）　🎧 MP3 **130**

情境 ❶

P What's Ghost Month?

鬼月是什麼啊？

D We feed the **spirits**[1]. The **ceremony**[2] is called Pudu.

我們會餵食鬼魂，那個儀式叫作普渡。

P Feed the spirits? That's interesting!

餵食鬼魂？好有趣啊！

D It's a **tradition**[3]. People care for the lonely ghosts, you know, the ghosts that do not have family.

這是一種傳統，人們照顧孤獨的鬼魂，你知道的，那些沒有家人的鬼魂。

情境 ❷

P I've seen a lot of **incense**[4] and **offerings**[5] around. Is there a festival?

我看到很多香和供品，是不是有什麼節慶？

D Yeah, it's Ghost Month. It's also called the Zhongyuan Festival.

是的，現在是鬼月，也叫作中元節。

P Are there any things I should avoid doing?

在這段時間裡我應該避免做什麼嗎？

D Some people avoid swimming or going out late at night.

有些人避免游泳或深夜外出。

★更多實用說法★　😄 MP3 **131**

司機

- It's our tradition.
  這是我們的傳統。

- In Taiwan, we **celebrate**[6] the Lunar New Year with family.
  在台灣，我們會跟家人一起慶祝農曆新年。

- During the Qingming Festival, we honor our **ancestors**[7].
  清明節時，我們向祖先致敬。

- During the Dragon Boat Festival, we eat Zongzi.
  在端午節，我們吃粽子。

- During the Hungry Ghost Festival, we give spirits food and burn incense.
  在中元節期間，我們給予鬼魂食物並燒香拜拜。

- Moon Festival is about moon cakes and family **reunions**[8].
  中秋節是關於月餅和家庭團聚的節日。

🔋 Word List　　　　　　　　　　　　　😄 MP3 **132**

1. spirit [ˈspɪrɪt] *n.* 靈魂；鬼魂
2. ceremony [ˈsɛrəˌmonɪ] *n.* 典禮；儀式
3. tradition [trəˈdɪʃən] *n.* 傳統
4. incense [ˈɪnsɛns] *n.* 香

5. offering [ˈɔfərɪŋ] *n.* 供品；祭品
6. celebrate [ˈsɛləˌbret] *v.* 慶祝
7. ancestor [ˈænsɛstə] *n.* 祖先
8. reunion [riˈjunjən] *n.* 團聚；聚會

情境 ❶

P Do you know any places for **nightlife**[1] in Taipei?

有沒有什麼地方可以體驗台北夜生活？

D There are many, like karaoke, sports bars, wine bars or live music bars. What are you into?

有很多耶，像是 KTV、運動酒吧、酒館或現場演奏酒吧。你喜歡哪一種？

P I'm up for anything fun. What's the drinking **culture**[2] like here?

我對所有好玩的事都感興趣。這裡的飲酒文化是怎樣的？

D It's hard to say. I think for many people, it's more about good vibes.

很難說。我覺得對很多人來說，重要的是歡樂的氛圍。

情境 ❷

P I've heard karaoke is a big thing here. Is it true?

我聽說 KTV 在這裡很受歡迎。是真的嗎？

D Umm, kind of, especially for young people. Having a party in KTV is popular.

嗯，算是吧，特別是對年輕人來說，在 KTV 開派對很受歡迎。

P Do Taiwanese people love barhopping?

台灣人喜歡酒吧一家連著一家續攤喝下去嗎？

D Not really. But we do have many pubs and bars. And sometimes it's ALL YOU CAN DRINK.

不太算是吧。不過真的有很多酒吧和夜店。有時候還可以無限暢飲喔。

★ 更多實用說法 ★　🎧 MP3 **134**

司機

- The **energy**³ goes up, when DJ plays EDM Music.
  當 DJ 播放電音舞曲的時候，氣氛變得很嗨。

- Xinyi District is a popular hub for nightlife.
  信義區是夜生活的熱門聚集地。

- If you are into Taipei's nightlife, you can go to Xinyi District.
  如果你對台北夜生活有興趣的話，你可以去信義區。

- Local bar-goers are usually **friendly**⁴.
  當地酒吧的客人通常都很友善。

- Most of them can speak English.
  他們大多數都能說英語。

Ch 3
萬用聊天話題

Word List　🎧 MP3 **135**

1. nightlife [ˈnaɪtˌlaɪf] *n.* 夜生活
2. culture [ˈkʌltʃə] *n.* 文化
3. energy [ˈɛnədʒɪ] *n.* 活力
4. friendly [ˈfrɛndlɪ] *adj.* 友好的；親切的

06 運動競賽

D → **Driver**（司機）　　**P** → **Passenger**（乘客）　🎧 MP3 **136**

情境 ①

D Are you a baseball **fan**[1]?

你是棒球迷嗎？

P No, I don't really **follow**[2] **sports**[3].

不是，我其實沒有很關注體育競賽。

情境 ②

D Do you like watching basketball **games**[4]?

你喜歡看籃球賽嗎？

P Of course I do!

當然喜歡啊！

D There are some sports bars downtown, and they have amazing game nights.

市區有一些運動酒吧，他們會辦一些令人驚豔的比賽之夜。

P Nice! Thanks for the recommendations.

太好了！謝謝推薦。

 Word List

1. fan [fæn] *n.* 愛好者
2. follow [ˋfɑlo] *v.* 關注；遵守
3. sport [sport] *n.* 運動
4. game [gem] *n.* 遊戲；競賽

★更多實用說法★ 🎧 MP3 **137**

司機

● Did you see the game last night?
你有看昨天那場球賽嗎？

● Are you following the World Cup?
你有在看世足賽嗎？

● Basketball games are always **exciting**[5].
籃球比賽總是令人振奮。

● Do you follow any **teams**[6] back home?
你有支持哪一個球隊嗎？

● Have you caught any baseball games in Taipei?
你在台北看過任何棒球比賽嗎？

● Do you play any sports?
你有玩任何運動嗎？

● I like tennis/badminton/pin-pong/swimming/fishing.
我喜歡網球 / 羽毛球 / 桌球 / 游泳 / 釣魚。

● Are you a football/soccer/baseball/basketball fan?
你是（美式）橄欖球 / 足球 / 棒球 / 籃球迷嗎？

🎧 MP3 **138**

5. exciting [ɪkˋsaɪtɪŋ] *adj.* 令人興奮的
6. team [tim] *n.* 隊；組

基本應對用語

🎧 MP3 **139**

☐ Where are you from?
你是哪裡人？

☐ Is it your first time in Taipei/Taiwan?
這是你第一次來到台北／台灣嗎？

☐ Your first time here?
這是你第一次來這裡嗎？

☐ What brings you to Taiwan?
你為什麼會來台灣呢？

☐ Are you on a business trip or just visiting?
你是來出差還是來旅遊呢？

☐ How long are you planning to stay?
你打算待多長時間？

☐ Have you been here before?
你有來過這裡嗎？

☐ How long have you been here?
你來這裡多久了？

☐ It's been nice chatting with you.
跟你聊天很開心。

☐ Enjoy your stay in Taiwan.
享受你在台灣的時光。

☐ Take care. Have a nice day!
保重，祝你有美好的一天！（用於道別時）

| D → **Driver**（司機） | P → **Passenger**（乘客） | 🎧 MP3 **140** |

D Where are you from?
你從哪裡來的？

P I'm from Japan.
我從日本來的。

D Is it your first time in Taipei?
這是你第一次來台北嗎？

P No, I've been here many times.
不是，我來台北好多次了。

D Your first time here?
你是第一次來這裡嗎？

P Yes, it is.
對，第一次。

D What brings you to Taiwan?
你為什麼會來台灣呢？

P I'm on vacation.
我來渡假。

D Are you on a business trip or just visiting?
你是來出差還是來旅遊呢？

P I'm here on business.
我來出差的。

D How long are you planning to stay?

你打算待多長時間？

P I plan to stay for two weeks.

我打算待兩週。

D How long have you been here?

你來這裡多久了？

P I've been here for five days.

我來五天了。

D It's been nice chatting with you.

跟你聊天很開心。

P Yeah, it's been great talking to you, too.

跟你聊天我也很開心。

D Have a nice day.

祝你有美好的一天。

P Thanks, you too.

謝謝，也祝你有美好的一天。

D Take care!

保重喔！

P Thanks, have a great one!

謝謝，祝你過得愉快！

Chapter 4

狀況發生

D → **Driver**（司機）　　P → **Passenger**（乘客）　　😵 MP3 **141**

情境 ❶

D How's it going? Where can I take you tonight?
你好嗎？今晚要去哪裡？

P Mmm ... I need to go home.
嗯……我要回家。

D Alright, I'll get you home safe. Can you please let me know your address?
好的，我會讓你安全回家。你可以告訴我你的地址嗎？

P It's uhh ... it's like ... um, 12 something Zhongxiao ..ast Road.
嗯……就是那個……那個……呃，12……什麼什麼忠孝懂路。

D Sorry, is it 12 Zhongxiao East Road?
抱歉，是忠孝東路 12 號嗎？

P Yeah, right.
對，沒錯。

情境 ❷

D Can you say your address one more time? Just want to make sure.
能再說一次你的地址嗎？想跟你確認一下。

P Uhh, it's umm ... 168 ... Section 2 ... North Zhongshan North ...
呃，是……嗯……168……二段……北、中山北……

D Is it 168, Section 2, Zhongshan North Road? Is that right?
是中山北路二段 168 號，對嗎？

P That's right.

對，沒錯。

D Got it. Let's get you there.

知道了。我把你送到那裡。

★更多實用說法★　😊 MP3 **142**

司機

● Hey, you doing okay back there?

嘿，你在後座還好嗎？

● I want to make sure we get you home safe.

我想確保我可以把你平安送回家。

● Can you repeat the address for me, just to **double-check**[1]?

你能重複一次地址嗎？我確認一下。

● If you need a **vomit**[2] bag, it's right by your side.

如果你需要嘔吐袋，它就在你旁邊。

● Hey, if you feel you're going to be **sick**[3], just give me a **heads-up**[4], okay?

嘿，如果你感覺要嘔吐，提前告訴我一聲，好嗎？

 Word List　😊 MP3 **143**

1. double-check [ˈdʌblˈtʃɛk] *v.* 複核
2. vomit [ˈvamɪt] *n.* 嘔吐
3. sick [sɪk] *adj.* 生病的；想嘔吐的
4. heads-up [ˈhɛdzˋʌp] *n.* 注意；提醒

127

情境 ❶

P I need to go to the hotel on Dunhua North Road.

我要去敦化北路的飯店。（有一點口音）

D Just want to make sure, you said the hotel on Dunhua North Road. It's MANDARIN ORIENTAL, TAIPEI, right?

確認一下，你說敦化北路的飯店，就是台北文華東方酒店，對吧？

P Yeah, you're right.

對，沒錯。

情境 ❷

D Sorry, can you please **repeat**[1] that?

抱歉，你能再說一次嗎？

P Sure, to Xinxin restaurant.

沒問題，到新星餐廳。

D Umm ... I don't know where it is. Are there any **landmarks**[2] near your destination?

嗯……我不知道那個地方在哪。你的目的地附近有沒有什麼地標？

🔖 Word List

1. repeat [rɪˋpit] *v.* 重複
2. landmark [ˋlænd͵mɑrk] *n.* 地標

P Oh, it's on Renai Road, and ... uhh, it's next to an ~~elementary~~ ~~school~~.

噢，它在仁愛路上，我想，呃，旁邊有一所小學。

D Got it! We'll ~~head to~~ Renai Road first.

知道了！我們先開往仁愛路。

★更多實用說法★　😵 MP3 **145**

司機

● Sorry, would you mind slowing down?
抱歉，可以說慢一點嗎？

● Would you mind repeating that?
可以重複一次嗎？

● Could you say that **again**[3], please?
能再說一次嗎？

● I want to make sure I got it right.
我想確認我聽的是正確的。

● Sorry, I didn't **catch**[4] that.
抱歉，我沒聽清楚。

😵 MP3 **146**

3. again [əˈgɛn] *adv.* 再一次
4. catch [kætʃ] *v.* 聽清楚

03 焦急慌亂的乘客

D → Driver（司機）　　**P** → Passenger（乘客）　　🎧 MP3 **147**

情境 ❶

P How long do you think it will take to get to Sun Yat-Sen Memorial Hall?

你覺得到國父紀念館要多久？

D It shouldn't take longer than thirty minutes.

應該不會超過三十分鐘。

情境 ❷

P We haven't moved in five minutes. I'm going to be late.

我們有五分鐘都沒有前進了。我要遲到了。

D Sorry, it's always like this during **peak**[1] hours.

抱歉，尖峰時段都是這樣。

 Word List

1. **peak** [pik] *adj.* 高峰的（時段）

★ 更多實用說法 ★　🎧 MP3 **148**

乘客

● You're driving too fast. It's **dangerous**[2].

你開得太快了，很危險。

● Did you see that? You almost hit that dog.

你有看到嗎？你差點撞到那隻狗。

● I'm feeling sick. Can you drive faster?

我不舒服。你能開快一點嗎？

司機

● If traffic isn't bad, then I can get you there in five minutes.

如果交通不擁擠，我們五分鐘就能到。

● Don't worry. Wasn't even close!

別擔心。完全沒事！（還差得遠呢）

● Hang on! We're almost at the hospital.

再堅持一下！我們快到醫院了。

🎧 MP3 **149**

2. dangerous [ˋdendʒərəs] *adj.* 危險的

D → **Driver**（司機）　　P → **Passenger**（乘客）　🎧 MP3 **150**

情境 ❶

P Uh, I need to go to ... um ... Minsheng Street? I think?

嗯，我需要去，嗯，民生街？我想是這樣吧？

D No worries! Minsheng Street, got it. Can you name a landmark close to your destination?

別擔心！民生街，了解。你可以說一個你的目的地附近的地標嗎？

P Um, I'm not sure. I think it's near Carrefour?

嗯，我不太確定。我想應該是家樂福附近？

D Okay! Let's head to that Carrefour first.

好！那我們先前往那間家樂福。

> **核心句型** 🎧 150-1
> Let's head to + 地點.

情境 ❷

P This isn't the right place.

這不是我要去的地方。

D Sorry, you said 128 Wenhua Road, and here we are.

不好意思，你剛才是說文化路 128 號，就是這裡。

P Oh, no, did I say Wenhua Road? I'm **supposed**[1] to be at Wenhua Street, not Road!

哎呀，我剛剛說文化路嗎？我是要去文化街，不是文化路！

D Ah, got it. That can be easy to mix up. No worries, I'll take you to Wenhua Street.

啊，了解。那很容易搞混，沒關係，我載你到文化街。

★ 更多實用說法 ★　🎧 MP3 **151**

司機

- Do you have an address?
  你有地址嗎？

- Any chance you remember the name of the restaurant?
  你有沒有可能記得那家餐廳的名字？

- Any chance you mean the one by the mall?
  你是不是指是在購物中心附近的那一家？

乘客

- I'll tell you where to go when we get closer.
  快到的時候我再告訴你詳細的地方。

- Just drive, and I'll let you know where to drop me off.
  就先開車，我會告訴你我要下車的地方。

- Head to downtown first. We'll **figure it out**[2] when we get closer.
  先往市區開，等我們靠近那邊一點再說。

🔋 Word List　🎧 MP3 **152**

1. supposed [sə`pozd] *adj.* 應該；應當
2. figure it out 弄懂；弄明白；想出

D → **Driver**（司機）　　P → **Passenger**（乘客）　🎧 MP3 **153**

情境 ❶

D Did you see that? There's an **ambulance**[1]. Some **drivers**[2] just don't **move**[3] for **emergency**[4] **vehicles**[5].

你有看到嗎？救護車在那邊。有些司機就不讓開。

P I don't get it! Drivers should really make way for them.

我真搞不懂！駕駛人應該為緊急情況讓路。

D Wonder why some people forget that.

真奇怪有些人為什麼會忘記這點。

情境 ❷

P There's a **siren**[6] behind us.

我們後面有鳴笛聲。

D Yeah, I heard that. I'm pulling off to the side of the road.

對啊，我聽到了，我要靠邊停一下。

Word List

1. ambulance [`ˈæmbjələns] *n.* 救護車
2. driver [`ˈdraɪvə] *n.* 駕駛人；司機
3. move [muv] *v.* 移動；離開
4. emergency [ɪˈmɝdʒənsɪ] *n.* 緊急情況
5. vehicle [`ˈviɪkl] *n.* 車輛
6. siren [`ˈsaɪrən] *n.* 警報器

 ★ 更多實用說法 ★　🚗 MP3 **154**

司機

- Drivers need to be always looking and listening.
  司機需要時刻保持警覺，留心四周。

- When you spot an ambulance, you pull over to the right side of the road.
  看到救護車時，要靠右停車。

- When a fire truck is **approaching**[7], you should pull over and stop.
  當有消防車靠近的時候，要靠邊暫停。

- Don't become a **roadblock**[8].
  千萬不要變成路障。

🚗 MP3 **155**

---

7. approach [ə`protʃ] *v.* 接近；靠近
8. roadblock [`rod.blɑk] *n.* 路障

06 遇到車禍

| D | → **Driver**（司機） | P | → **Passenger**（乘客） | ☺ MP3 **156** |

情境 ❶

D It looks like a **fender-bender**[1] up ahead.

前面好像有小擦撞。

P Oh no, I hope everyone's okay.

噢不，希望大家都平安。

> 核心句型 ☺ 156-1
> I hope ...

情境 ❷

D Uh-oh, looks like there's an **accident**[2].

噢喔，看起來好像是車禍。

P What happened?

怎麼一回事？

D Not sure, but it's **causing**[3] a traffic jam. The road's a parking lot now.

不確定，但是現在整個塞車，這條路就像是個停車場一樣。

🗊 Word List

1. fender-bender [ˈfɛndəˈbɛndə] *n.* 小擦撞；不嚴重的車禍事故
2. accident [ˈæksədənt] *n.* 意外；事故
3. cause [kɔz] *v.* 造成；導致

★更多實用說法★ 🎧 MP3 **157**

司機

- It's bumper to bumper. Must be a **crash**[4] **somewhere**[5].
  車子（一輛緊跟著一輛）塞成這樣，前面一定不知道哪裡有車禍。

- Looks like a head-on **collision**[6].
  看起來像是正面對撞。

- It was a rear-end collision.
  追撞。

- We should wait for the police.
  我們應該等警察來。

- Luckily, no one is hurt.
  好險，沒有人受傷。

🎧 MP3 **158**

4. crash [kræʃ] *n.* 相撞（事故）
5. somewhere [ˈsʌmˌhwɛr] *adv.* 在某處
6. collision [kəˈlɪʒən] *n.* （車輛的）碰撞；相撞

07 遇到「馬路三寶」

D → **Driver**（司機）　　P → **Passenger**（乘客）　😊 MP3 **159**

情境 ❶

D Did you see that? That guy cut me off!

你看到了嗎？他就這樣切到我前面！

P That driver must be in a hurry to get somewhere.

那位司機肯定是趕著去某個地方。

情境 ❷

P Passing like that is dangerous. That was close!

像那樣超車真危險。好驚險！

D Yeah! I felt like I was in a movie.

是啊！感覺就像在演一場電影。

P **Jaywalkers**[1] have also been a problem.

行人穿越馬路也是個大問題。

D I know what you mean.

我知道你的意思。

 Word List

1. jaywalker [ˈdʒeˌwɔkə] *n.* 亂穿越馬路的人

★ 更多實用說法 ★   🔊 MP3 **160**

司機

● **Safety**[2] first.
安全第一。

● What's going on today?
今天是發生什麼事了？

● Cutting people off should be an Olympic sport for some drivers.
對某些司機來說，超車應該算是一項奧運比賽項目。

● The **cyclist**[3] went the wrong way. That's dangerous!
那個騎自行車的人逆向，很危險耶！

● That driver just ran a red light! Did you see that?
那台車剛剛闖紅燈！你有看到嗎？

● Not following traffic rules is very dangerous.
不遵守交通規則是很危險的。

🔊 MP3 **161**

2. **safety** [ˈseftɪ] *n.* 安全   3. **cyclist** [ˈsaɪklɪst] *n.* 自行車騎士

08 遇到拖吊

D → **Driver**（司機）　　P → **Passenger**（乘客）　😵 MP3 **162**

情境 ❶

P Look over there! The car is about to get **towed**[1].

看那邊！那輛車快要被拖走了。

D Yup, in Taiwan, a red line on the **roadside**[2] means no parking.

是的，在台灣，路邊的紅線表示禁止停車。

情境 ❷

P Just **curious**[3], is the **fine**[4] here expensive?

只是好奇，你們這邊罰款貴不貴？

D Oh, a bit, yeah. If your car gets towed, you'll have to pay the fine and the towing fee.

噢，是有點貴。如果你的車被拖走了，你要支付罰款，還有拖吊費用。

 Word List

1. tow [to] *v.* 拖；拉
2. roadside [ˋrod͵saɪd] *n.* 路邊
3. curious [ˋkjʊrɪəs] *adj.* 好奇的
4. fine [faɪn] *n.* 罰金

★ 更多實用說法 ★　🔊 MP3 **163**

司機

● Someone's in trouble for parking on the yellow line.
有人因為停黃線要惹上麻煩了。

● See that tow **truck**[5] and the **police**[6]? They're **serious**[7] about those red lines.
你有看到那輛拖吊車和警察嗎？他們對那些紅線可是認真的。

● Parking on the red line is a big no-no.
千萬不要紅線違規停車。

乘客

● Looks like someone didn't follow the **rules**[8].
看來有人沒有遵守規定。

● Red line means no parking, right?
紅線表示禁止停車，對吧？

🔊 MP3 **164**

5. truck [trʌk] *n.* 卡車
6. police [pəˈlis] *n.* 警察
7. serious [ˈsɪrɪəs] *adj.* 認真的；嚴重的
8. rule [rul] *n.* 規則

09 遇到臨檢

D → **Driver**（司機）　　**P** → **Passenger**（乘客）　🎧 MP3 **165**

情境 ❶

D Oh, there's a **checkpoint**[1]. We need to pull over for a moment.

噢，警察在進行臨檢。我們需要暫時停車一下。

P Sure, no problem.

當然，沒問題。

情境 ❷

D There's a DUI checkpoint up ahead.

前面有酒測。

P Is this **common**[2] in Taiwan?

這在台灣常見嗎？

D Yeah, kind of, drunk driving is still a big problem here.

嗯，算蠻常見的，酒駕在這裡依然是一個大問題。

 Word List

1. checkpoint [ˈtʃɛkˌpɔɪnt] *n.* 檢查站
2. common [ˈkɑmən] *adj.* 常見的；普通的

★ 更多實用說法 ★　🔊 MP3 **166**

司機

● There's a roadside check up ahead.
前面有路邊檢查點。

● If they suspect you've been drinking, they can **ask for** an **alcohol**[3] breath test.
如果他們懷疑你有喝酒，他們可以要求進行酒精呼氣測試。

● Sometimes, the police do routine checks.
有時候，警方會進行例行檢查。

● In serious cases, you may face fines or even a **license**[4] suspension.
在嚴重的情況下，你可能會被罰款，甚至有可能被吊銷駕照。

🔊 MP3 **167**

3. alcohol [ˈælkəˌhɔl] *n.* 酒精
4. license [ˈlaɪsns] *n.* 許可證；執照

143

10 車子故障

D → **Driver**（司機）　　P → **Passenger**（乘客）　　MP3 **168**

情境 ❶

D Sorry about this, but something is wrong with the car. I'm pulling over.

不好意思，但車子出了點問題。我靠邊停一下。

P What's that **smell**[1]? What's the problem?

那是什麼味道？出了什麼問題？

D Not sure, something went wrong with the **engine**[2]. I need to call a tow truck.

不太確定，引擎似乎出了點問題。我打電話叫拖吊車。

情境 ❷

P What's that noise under the car?

車底下是什麼聲音？

D I'm not sure. Let me pull over and check it out.

我也不太確定。我靠邊停車來檢查一下。

情境 ❸

P Hey! Something just fell out of the trunk!

嘿！東西從後車廂裡掉出來了！

D Oh no, really? Let me pull over.

噢不，真的嗎？讓我找個地方停下來。

★ 更多實用說法 ★ 　 🎧 MP3 **169**

司機

- I'm sorry, but we seem to have a flat tire.
  抱歉，但我的車好像爆胎了。

- Smells like something is **burning**[3]. I'm pulling over.
  有個什麼東西燒焦的味道，我靠邊停一下。

- I'll try to restart the car, but it may take a moment.
  我試試看重新啟動車子，但可能需要一點時間。

- Looks like a **battery**[4] issue. I'll call a tow truck.
  看起來好像是電池問題，我打電話請拖吊車。

- There's a strange noise from the engine.
  引擎發出奇怪的聲音。

- Oh no, I think I'm out of gas. I'll need to find a gas station.
  噢不，車子沒油了，我要找個加油站。

- Sorry, I think I just **ran over**[5] something.
  抱歉，我想我剛剛輾過什麼東西。

- I'll pull over and check what's going on.
  我要靠邊停一下，看看發生了什麼事。

Ch 4

狀況發生

Word List　　　　　　　　　　　　🎧 MP3 **170**

1. **smell** [smɛl] *n./v.* 氣味；聞起來有……的氣味
2. **engine** [ˋɛndʒən] *n.* 引擎
3. **burning** [ˋbɜnɪŋ] *adj.* 燃燒的
4. **battery** [ˋbætərɪ] *n.* 電池
5. **run over** 輾過

基本應對用語

☐ Do you think we can make it in twenty minutes?
你覺得二十分鐘之內我們可以抵達目的地嗎？

☐ Do you think we can make it to SOGO in ten minutes?
你覺得十分鐘之內我們可以到 SOGO 嗎？

☐ Could you please drive a bit slower?
你可以稍微開慢一點嗎？

☐ Can you drive faster? I need to be there in five minutes.
你可以開快一點嗎？我得在五分鐘之內抵達目的地。

☐ No, that's not what I said. I said Wenhua Street, not Road!
不是，我剛剛不是那樣說的，我說的是文化街，不是路！

☐ I'm not sure about the address, but it's somewhere near Taipei City Hall.
地址我不太確定，但大概在台北市政府附近。

☐ I don't have the exact address, but it's close to Taipei City Hospital.
我沒有確切的地址，但靠近台北市立聯合醫院。

☐ The traffic is crazy. Is it always like this?
這個路況太驚人了。平常都這樣嗎？

☐ Someone needs to tell that driver to slow down. That's too dangerous.
應該要有人去跟那個駕駛說開慢一點。太危險了。

☐ No worries, take your time.
不急，慢慢來。

司機　🚗 MP3 **172**

☐ Take it easy. If traffic isn't bad, I can take you there in ten minutes.
別擔心。如果路況不錯，十分鐘之內我們就會到。

☐ Don't worry. We'll be there by 2:30. You'll make it.
別擔心，我們會在兩點半之前到，你趕得上的。

☐ Could you confirm the address again?
你能再確認一下地址嗎？

☐ I'm not familiar with that place. Do you have the address or can you tell me how to get there?
我對那個地方不太熟悉。你有地址嗎？或者能告訴我該如何到達嗎？

☐ Sorry, there's something wrong with my car.
抱歉，我的車出了些問題。

☐ I need to pull over and call a tow truck.
我需要靠邊停並打電話叫拖吊車。

☐ There's a fire truck coming through. I'm pulling over.
有一輛消防車要過，我靠邊停一下。

☐ There's a lot of traffic at this time of day.
這個時間車很多。

☐ Looks like there's a police checkpoint up ahead.
前面好像有警察臨檢。

☐ They're checking for drunk driving.
他們在做酒測。

Notes

Chapter 5

Uber 專區

D → **Driver**（司機）　　P → **Passenger**（乘客）　　🎧 MP3 **173**

情境 ❶

D Are you Justin Smith?

請問是賈斯丁・史密斯嗎？

P Yes.

我是。

D The destination is Yehliu, right?

你是要去野柳，對吧？

P That's **correct**[1].

沒錯。

情境 ❷

D Hi, did you **request**[2] an Uber?

嗨，你有叫 Uber 嗎？

P Yes, to Taipei Medical University Hospital.

對，我要到台北醫學大學附設醫院。

D Sure! The **traffic**[3] is good today, and the **journey**[4] should take about twelve minutes.

好的！今天交通狀況蠻好的，車程大約十二分鐘。

🔲 Word List

1. **correct** [kəˋrɛkt] *adj.* 正確的；對的
2. **request** [rɪˋkwɛst] *v.* 請求；要求
3. **traffic** [ˋtræfɪk] *n.* 交通（量）
4. **journey** [ˋdʒɝnɪ] *n.* 旅程；路程

★ 更多實用說法 ★　　🎧 MP3 **174**

司機

● Is your destination National Taiwan University **Hospital**[5]?
你是要去台大醫院嗎？

● Are you going to Regent Taipei?
你是要去台北晶華酒店嗎？

● Is your final stop Hsing Tian Kong?
你是要去行天宮嗎？

● **Fasten**[6] your **seatbelt**[7], please.
請繫上安全帶，謝謝。

乘客

● Yeah, that's right.
對，沒錯。

● **Exactly**[8].
正確無誤。

● You're correct.
正確。

🎧 MP3 **175**

5. hospital [ˈhɑspɪtl] *n.* 醫院
6. fasten [ˈfæsn] *v.* 扣緊；繫緊
7. seatbelt [ˈsitˌbɛlt] *n.* 安全帶
8. exactly [ɪgˈzæktlɪ] *adv.* 完全準確地

D → **Driver**（司機）　P → **Passenger**（乘客）　☺ MP3 **176**

情境 ❶

D Hi, this is your Uber driver. I'm **currently**[1] at Meeting Point 4. Where are you?

嗨，我是 Uber 司機，我在會面點 4 這裡，你在哪裡呢？

P I'm right here, but I don't see your car.

我就在這啊，但我沒看到你的車。

D The license plate is ABC-9999, and it's a black TOYOTA.

我的車牌是 ABC-9999，是一輛黑色的 TOYOTA。

P I'm right under the Meeting Point 4. I'm wearing a red jacket.

我就站在會面點 4 牌子的下面。我穿一件紅色外套。

D Wait, I see you.

等等，我看到你了。

情境 ❷

D Could you please walk to West Gate 3? That's the only place I can pick you up.

可以麻煩你走到西三門嗎？只有這邊可以上車。

P Oh, okay. Just wait for me.

噢，好，等我一下。

 Word List

1. currently [ˈkɜəntlɪ] *adv.* 目前；現在

★ 更多實用說法 ★　⊕ MP3 **177**

司機

- I can't park here.
  這邊不能停車。

- You can **reserve**[2] a ride in advance.
  你可以提前預約 Uber。

- You can request a ride before your flight.
  你可以在搭飛機前預約 Uber。

- The pickup location is outside the Arrivals Hall.
  上車點在入境大廳外面。

- You can pick a meeting point from your Uber app.
  你可以在 Uber 應用程式裡面選擇一個會面點。

- You can only pick up **passengers**[3] in the pickup zone.
  只有載客區可以讓乘客上車。

- This area is for drop-offs only. No parking.
  這個地方只能讓乘客下車。不能臨停。

乘客

- Taipei Main Station is a maze.
  台北車站像是一個迷宮。

⊕ MP3 **178**

---

2. **reserve** [rɪˈzɝv] *v.* 預約；預訂　　　3. **passenger** [ˈpæsndʒɚ] *n.* 乘客

D → **Driver**（司機）　P → **Passenger**（乘客）　 MP3 **179**

情境 ❶

D Here we are.
我們到囉。

P Umm, are you sure this is the right place?
嗯，你確定是這個地方嗎？

D Let's check the destination you put in first, okay? It's 14 Songzhi Road, right?
我們先確認一下你輸入的地址好嗎？地址是松智路 14 號，對嗎？

P Yeah, but ... oh no ... I was given the wrong address.
對啊，但是……噢天哪……他們給我的地址是錯的。

情境 ❷

P Wait, this isn't the place I want to go to.
欸，這不是我要去的地方耶。

D No problem. Could you confirm the correct address for me?
沒問題。你幫我確認一下正確的地址好嗎？

P Oops, it seems I made a **mistake**[1]. It should be Wenhua Road, not Street.
哎呀，看來是我弄錯了。我要去的地方應該是文化路，不是文化街。

🔖 Word List

1. mistake [mɪˋstek] *n.* 錯誤

★ 更多實用說法 ★ 🎧 MP3 **180**

司機

● Hi, I'm Jenny Chen. You're going to 123 Dongmen Street. Is that right?
嗨，我是 Jenny Chen。你要去東門街 123 號，對嗎？

● Who's your driver?
你的司機是？

● When I pick someone up, I always **confirm**[2] the name and the address.
每次要載客人時，我都會先確認名字和地址。

● Let me double-check the address on the app.
我再確認一下應用程式上的地址。

乘客

● Who are you here to pick up?
你是來接誰的？

● Can I change the destination on the Uber app?
我可以在 Uber 應用程式上更改目的地嗎？

● The address showed up correctly, but the **pin**[3] was wrong.
地址那時候顯示是正確的，但是標記位置錯了。

🎧 MP3 **181**

2. confirm [kənˋfɝm] *v.* 確認

3. pin [pɪn] *n.*（定位）大頭針

04 乘客欲臨時增加停靠點

D → **Driver**（司機）　　P → **Passenger**（乘客）　　🎧 MP3 **182**

情境 ①

P Excuse me, I want to make a quick stop. Do you know how I do that?

打擾一下，我想要新增一個停靠點。你知道要怎麼操作嗎？

D Oh, that's easy. You can just tap 'Where to' and **enter**[1] a new address. The fare will be **recalculated**[2].

噢，很簡單。你只須點一下「要去哪裡」，然後輸入新的地址。車資會重新計算。

情境 ②

D Good morning, you're going to Sheraton Hotel, right?

早安，你要去喜來登大飯店，對嗎？

P Yes, and I also need to add a stop to pick up my friend.

是的，然後我還需要增加一個停靠點，去接我的朋友。

D No problem. Just tap the Plus (+) to the right of the 'Where to' box.

沒問題。點「要去哪裡」框框右側的那個加號（+）就可以。

 Word List

1. enter [ˈɛntə] *v.* 輸入
2. recalculate [riˈkælkjəˌlet] *v.* 重新計算

★ 更多實用說法 ★　🔊 MP3 **183**

乘客

● Can we make a quick stop at Cosmos Hotel Taipei?
我們可以在天成大飯店先停一下嗎？

司機

● You can drag your pin to another location on the **map**[3].
你可以在地圖上拖曳標記另一個地點。

● You can **add**[4] a stop during your Uber ride.
你可以在 Uber 行程中新增一個停靠點。

● You can add up to five extra stops.
最多可以新增五個停靠點。

● Tap 'Where to' first, and tap Plus (+) next to the destination box.
先點「要去哪裡？」，然後再點目的地框框旁邊的（+）。

● You can easily add, change, or **remove**[5] **additional**[6] stops during a ride.
你可以在行程中輕鬆新增、更改或移除額外停靠點。

● Just so you know, your fare will change.
只是提醒你，你的費用會有所變動。

🔊 MP3 **184**

---

3. map [mæp] *n.* 地圖
4. add [æd] *v.* 增加

5. remove [rɪˋmuv] *v.* 移除
6. additional [əˋdɪʃənl] *adj.* 額外的

基本應對用語

☐ Hi, this is your Uber driver.
嗨，我是你的 Uber 司機。

☐ Are you Ashley Walker?
你是艾許莉・沃克嗎？

☐ Are you going to Sanxia Old Street?
你是要前往三峽老街對嗎？

☐ Is the temperature okay for you?
車內的溫度對你來說還可以嗎？

☐ If you need any adjustments, feel free to let me know.
如果你需要調整什麼，隨時告訴我。

☐ We should reach your destination in about twenty minutes.
我們應該在大約二十分鐘之內到達你的目的地。

〈如有簡訊需求〉

☐ Hey, it's your Uber driver. I'm outside.
嗨，我是 Uber 司機。我已經在外面了。

☐ I'm at the pickup location.
我已經在指定上車地點了。

☐ Got it! I'll wait for you.
好的！我會等你。

| D | → **Driver**（司機） | P | → **Passenger**（乘客） | 🎧 MP3 **186** |

D How are you? Are you Mr. Ohtani?
你好，你是大谷先生嗎？

P Yes, I am.
是的，我是。

D Is your final stop Taoyuan Airport?
你是要到桃園機場對嗎？

P Yes.
是的。

D If you need any adjustments, feel free to let me know.
如果你需要調整什麼，隨時告訴我。

P Thanks, I'll let you know if I need anything.
謝謝，如果我需要什麼，我會告訴你的。

D We should reach your destination in about forty minutes.
我們應該可以在四十分鐘之內到達你的目的地。

P Okay, thanks for letting me know.
好，謝謝你告訴我。

D Here we are. Goodbye and take care.
我們到囉。再見，保重。

P Thank you. Have a great day.
謝謝，祝你有美好的一天。

Notes

Appendix

英文加油站

TAXI FARE (Daytime)
6:00 am to 11:00 pm
within 1.25 km: NT$85
over 1.25 km: NT$5 per 200 m
waiting: NT$5 per 60 seconds
(Taipei–Keelung metropolitan area)

計程車運價（日間）
凌晨六點到夜間十一點
1.25 公里內：台幣 85 元
1.25 公里以上：每 200 公尺 5 元
延滯計時：每 60 秒 5 元
（大台北地區）

★ 更多實用說法 ★　　🎧 MP3 **187**

乘客

● Do you **charge**¹ a flat rate? 你是定額收費（均一價）嗎？

司機

● It's metered. 我是按跳錶收費的。

● The initial charge is NT$85 for the first 1.25 km.
起步價為台幣八十五元，包含前 1.25 公里。

● After that, there's an **extra**² NT$5 for every 200 meters.
此後，每行駛二百公尺加收台幣五元。

● If you take a taxi between 11 pm and 6 am, there will be a
NT$20 **surcharge**³.
如果你是夜間十一點到清晨六點搭車，會額外多收台幣二十元費用。

★ 車資 (fare) 補充 ★

起步價	base fare
等候時間費	waiting time fee
夜間加成	nighttime surcharge
里程計價費率	metered fare
尖峰時間	rush hour

Word List　　　　　　　　　　🎧 MP3 **188**

1. charge [tʃɑrdʒ] *v./n.* 收費；費用

2. extra [ˈɛkstrə] *n./adj.* 附加費用；額外的

3. surcharge [ˈsɝˌtʃɑrdʒ] *n.* 額外費用

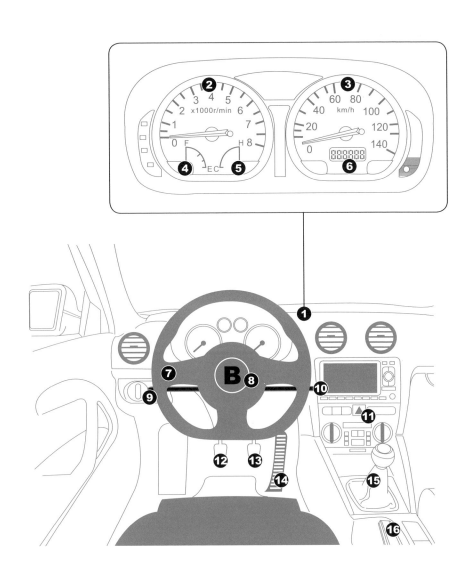

 Word List   ☎ MP3 **189**

1. dashboard [ˋdæʃˌbɔrd] 儀表板
2. tachometer [təˋkamətə] 轉速表
3. speedometer [spiˋdamətə] 車速表
4. gas gauge 油表
5. temperature gauge 溫度表
6. odometer [oˋdamətə] 里程表
7. steering wheel 方向盤
8. horn [hɔrn] 喇叭
9. (windshield) wiper switch 雨刷開關
10. turn signal switch 方向燈
11. hazard warning light switch 警示燈
12. clutch pedal 離合器
13. brake pedal 煞車
14. gas pedal / accelerator [ækˋsɛləˌretə] 油門；加速器
15. gearshift [ˋgɪrˌʃɪft] 排檔桿
16. parking brake 手煞車

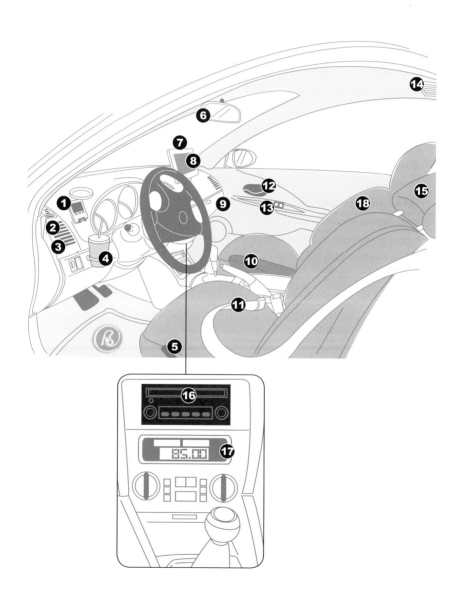

 Word List 🎧 MP3 **190**

1. global positioning system GPS 導航
2. heater [ˋhitɚ] 暖氣
3. air conditioning 空調（簡稱 A/C）
4. drink holder 飲料架
5. seat adjustment lever 座椅調整桿
6. rearview mirror 車內後視鏡
7. autonomous driving system 自動駕駛系統
8. touchscreen display 中控／觸控螢幕
9. glove box 前座置物箱
10. armrest [ˋarm‚rɛst] 扶手
11. seatbelt [ˋsit‚bɛlt] 安全帶
12. door handle 門把
13. window control 車窗開關
14. cabin light 車頂室內燈
15. headrest [ˋhɛd‚rɛst] 頸枕
16. radio [ˋredɪo] 廣播電台
17. meter [ˋmitɚ] 計費錶
18. front seat 前座／ back seat 後座

★ 更多實用說法 ★ 🎧 MP3 **191**

○ Don't forget to put on your seatbelt.
別忘了繫好安全帶。

○ Don't forget to buckle up for a safe ride.
為了行車安全，別忘了繫好安全帶。

○ If you want to move the seat back, just pull the lever on the side.
如果你要把座椅往後調整的話，只要拉旁邊的桿子就可以了。

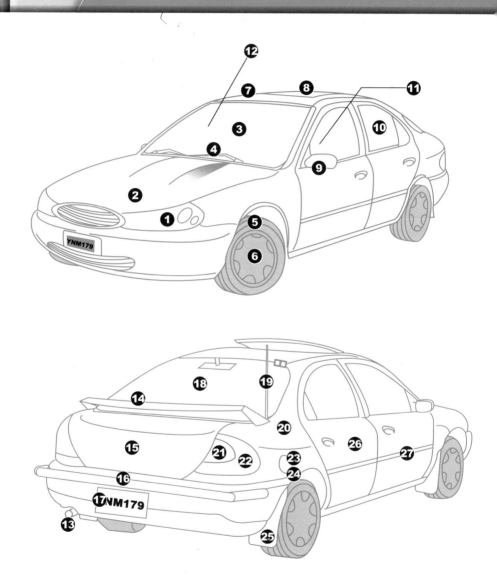

Word List

1. headlight [ˈhɛdˌlaɪt] 前燈
2. hood [hʊd] 引擎蓋
3. windshield [ˈwɪndˌʃild] 擋風玻璃
4. windshield wiper 擋風玻璃雨刷
5. tire [taɪr] 輪胎
6. wheel [hwil] 輪圈
7. roof [ruf] 車頂
8. sunroof [ˈsʌnˌruf] 天窗
9. side mirror 側後視鏡
10. rear-side window 後座側窗
11. driver side 駕駛側
12. passenger side 前座乘客側
13. tailpipe [ˈtelpaɪp] / exhaust pipe 排氣管
14. spoiler [ˈspɔɪlɚ] 擾流板
15. trunk [trʌŋk] 後車廂
16. bumper [ˈbʌmpɚ] 保險桿
17. license plate 車牌
18. rear window 後車窗
19. antenna [ænˈtɛnə] 天線
20. body panel 車身面板
21. reverse light 倒車燈
22. taillight [ˈtelˌlaɪt] 尾燈
23. gas cap 油箱蓋
24. fuel door 油箱外蓋
25. fender [ˈfɛndɚ] / mudflap [ˈmʌdˌflæp] 擋泥板
26. door [dor] 車門
27. trim [trɪm] 車身飾板

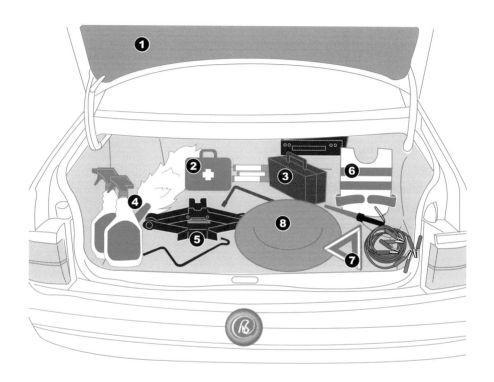

⛽ Word List   🎧 MP3 **193**

1. trunk lid 後車廂蓋
2. first-aid kit 急救箱
3. tool kit 工具箱
4. cleaning supplies〔複數形〕清潔用品
5. jack [dʒæk] 千斤頂
6. traffic vest 反光背心
7. warning triangle 三角警示牌
8. spare tire 備胎

★ 更多實用說法 ★   MP3 **194**

司機

● Just a moment, please. I've got a lot of **stuff**[1] in here. Let me make some room.

請稍等一下，我這邊放了很多東西，我挪個位置出來。

● Let me move the tool kit over to make room for your luggage.

我把這個工具箱移過去一點來放你的行李。

● I've got a flat tire. Give me a few minutes. I'll put on the spare tire.

我的輪胎爆胎了。給我幾分鐘，我換個備胎。

乘客

● Excuse me, you forgot to close your **fuel**[2] door.

不好意思，你忘記關油箱外蓋了。

● Do you have a first-aid kit?

請問你有急救箱嗎？

 Word List   MP3 **195**

1. stuff [stʌf] *n.* 物品；東西
2. fuel [`fjʊəl] *n.* 燃料

1. windshield washer fluid bottle 雨刷水箱
2. radiator overflow tank 副水箱
3. automatic transmission 自動變速器（簡稱 AT）
4. alternator [ˋɔltəˏnetə] 交流發電機
5. radiator [ˋredɪˏetə] 散熱器
6. grille [grɪl] 水箱護罩

7. spark plug 火星塞
8. spark plug wire 火星塞線
9. valve cover 汽缸蓋
10. oil filler cap 機油蓋
11. air cleaner 空氣清淨機
12. battery [ˋbætərɪ] 電瓶
13. fuse box / fuse panel 保險絲座

範例

中文地址：台北市信義區忠孝東路五段 123 號

英文地址：No. 123, Section 5, Zhongxiao East Road,
Xinyi District, Taipei City

說明

1. 中文地址是由大範圍到小範圍依序說明，但英文地址正好相反，是由小範圍到大範圍。

2. 門牌號碼，以「123」號為例，要說 No. 123；路段，以「五段」為例，要說 Section 5，語序與中文相反。

3. 號碼的口語表達習慣：以「忠孝東路 158 號」為例，英文口語會說「one fifty eight Zhongxiao East Road」或「one five eight Zhongxiao East Road」，而不會唸成「one hundred fifty eight（一百五十八）」。假如門牌號碼是四位數，則可拆成兩位數一組讀，以「1688 號」為例，會唸成「sixteen eighty-eight」。如果號碼是三位數，而中間數字是零，例如「302」，會唸成「three – oh（歐）– two」。

Word List　　　　　　　　　　　　　MP3 **197**

1. 樓層 floor [flor]
2. 號碼 number [ˈnʌmbɚ]
3. 弄 alley [ˈælɪ]
4. 巷 lane [len]
5. 街 street [strit]
6. 大道 boulevard [ˈbuləˌvɑrd]
7. 路 road [rod]
8. 村 village [ˈvɪlɪdʒ]
9. 鄉 / 鎮 township [ˈtaʊnʃɪp]
10. 區 district [ˈdɪstrɪkt]
11. 縣 county [ˈkaʊntɪ]
12. 市 city [ˈsɪtɪ]

08 常見建築物 / 地點 / 道路設施

 Word List

MP3 **198**

1. airport [ˈɛr‚port] 機場
2. bakery [ˈbekərɪ] 麵包店
3. bank [bæŋk] 銀行
4. bookstore [ˈbʊk‚stor] 書店
5. bridge [brɪdʒ] 橋
6. bus stop 公車站牌
7. café [kəˈfe] 咖啡廳
8. church [tʃɝtʃ] 教堂
9. cinema [ˈsɪnəmə] 電影院
10. clinic [ˈklɪnɪk] 診所
11. convenience store 便利商店
12. crosswalk [ˈkrɔs‚wɔk] 斑馬線
13. department store 百貨公司
14. diner [ˈdaɪnə] 小餐館
15. elevated highway 高架快速道路
16. fire station 消防局
17. footbridge [ˈfʊt‚brɪdʒ] 天橋
18. gallery [ˈgælərɪ] 畫廊
19. gas station 加油站
20. gym [dʒɪm] 健身房
21. hospital [ˈhɑspɪtl] 醫院
22. hotel [hoˈtɛl] 旅館
23. interchange [ˈɪntə‚tʃendʒ] 交流道
24. intersection [‚ɪntəˈsɛkʃən] 十字路口
25. library [ˈlaɪ‚brɛrɪ] 圖書館
26. museum [mjuˈzɪəm] 博物館
27. overpass [ˈovə‚pæs] 高架橋
28. park [pɑrk] 公園
29. pharmacy [ˈfɑrməsɪ] 藥局
30. police station 警察局
31. post office 郵局
32. restaurant [ˈrɛstərənt] 餐廳
33. school [skul] 學校
34. shopping mall 購物中心
35. stadium [ˈstedɪəm] 體育場；運動場
36. supermarket [ˈsupə‚mɑrkɪt] 超市
37. temple [ˈtɛmpl] 寺廟
38. traffic light 紅綠燈
39. train station 火車站
40. underpass [ˈʌndə‚pæs] 地下通道
41. World Trade Center 世貿中心
42. zebra crossing 斑馬線

Word List

MP3 **199**

1	one [wʌn]	50	fifty [ˈfɪftɪ]
2	two [tu]	60	sixty [ˈsɪkstɪ]
3	three [θri]	70	seventy [ˈsɛvntɪ]
4	four [fɔr]	80	eighty [ˈetɪ]
5	five [faɪv]	90	ninety [ˈnaɪntɪ]
6	six [sɪks]	100	hundred [ˈhʌndrəd]
7	seven [ˈsɛvn]	1000	thousand [ˈθaʊznd]
8	eight [et]	105	one hundred and five
9	nine [naɪn]	210	two hundred and ten
10	ten [tɛn]	315	three hundred and fifteen
11	eleven [ɪˈlɛvn]	365	three hundred and sixty five
12	twelve [twɛlv]	450	four hundred and fifty
13	thirteen [ˈθɝtin]	520	five hundred and twenty
14	fourteen [ˈforˈtin]	680	six hundred and eighty
15	fifteen [ˈfɪfˈtin]	795	seven hundred and ninety five
16	sixteen [ˈsɪksˈtin]	890	eight hundred and ninety
17	seventeen [ˌsɛvnˈtin]	930	nine hundred and thirty
18	eighteen [ˈeˈtin]	1005	one thousand and five
19	nineteen [ˈnaɪnˈtin]	1200	one thousand two hundred
20	twenty [ˈtwɛntɪ]	1350	one thousand three hundred and fifty
30	thirty [ˈθɝtɪ]		
40	forty [ˈfɔrtɪ]	2400	two thousand four hundred

注意 hundred 和 thousand 不需要加 "s"。

No Entry
禁止進入

 No Parking
禁止停車

 No U-turn
禁止迴轉

 Speed Limit: 60
最高速限 60 公里

 One Way
單行道

 No Left Turn
禁止左轉

 No Right Turn
禁止右轉

 No Overtaking[1]
禁止超車

 Roundabout / Traffic Circle
圓環

 Danger / Caution[2]
危險

 T-intersection
岔路

 Slow
慢行

 Word List
🔊 MP3 **200**

1. **overtake** [ˌovəˈtek] *v.* 超車

2. **caution** [ˈkɔʃən] *n.* 謹慎；小心

Notes

國家圖書館出版品預行編目（CIP）資料

雙語計程車英文句典 = Overheard in a taxi / 劉怡均編著. --
初版. -- 臺北市：波斯納出版有限公司, 2024.04
　　面；　公分
　　ISBN 978-626-98215-5-6（平裝）

1. CST：英語　2. CST：會話　3. CST：計程車

805.188   113001700

雙語計程車英文句典
Overheard in a Taxi

編　　著／劉怡均
執行編輯／游玉旻

出　　版／波斯納出版有限公司
地　　址／100 台北市館前路 26 號 6 樓
電　　話／(02) 2314-2525
傳　　真／(02) 2312-3535
客服專線／(02) 2314-3535
客服信箱／btservice@betamedia.com.tw
郵撥帳號／19493777
帳戶名稱／波斯納出版有限公司

總 經 銷／時報文化出版企業股份有限公司
地　　址／桃園市龜山區萬壽路二段 351 號
電　　話／(02) 2306-6842

出版日期／2024 年 4 月初版一刷
定　　價／350 元
Ｉ Ｓ Ｂ Ｎ／978-626-98215-5-6

Ⓑ 貝塔網址：www.betamedia.com.tw

喚醒你的英文語感！

Get a Feel for English !